Alpha Billionaire Club Boxed Set

J.L. Ryan

Published by J.L. Ryan, 2018.

ALPHA BILLIONAIRE CLUB BOXED SET

First edition. June 1, 2018.

Copyright © 2018 J.L. Ryan.

ISBN: 978-1393273189

Written by J.L. Ryan.

Also by J.L. Ryan

Alpha Billionaire Club Boxed Set
Bad Boy Billionaire Boxed Set
Billionaire Obsession
Billionaire Protector
Billionaire Scandal
Irresistible: A 7-Book Billionaire Romance Boxed Set
Owned by the Billionaire: A 5-Book Billionaire Romance Boxed Set
Plus Size Romance: A 9-Book Billionaire Romance Boxed Set
The Billionaire's Offer
Billionaires and Bad Boys
Billionaire Unleashed Boxed Set Series
Billionaire Unloved
Seduced by the Billionaire: A 5-Book Boxed Set
The Billionaire CEO: 4-Book Boxed Set
Curvy Romance
The Billionaire's Gift
The Billionaire Boss
Heart Of The Billionaire
BBW Romance
Baby For The Billionaire
Alpha Male Romances: 4-Book Boxed Set
BBW Curvy Romance: A 16-Book Boxed Set
BBW Romance
BBW Romance With Billionaires Box Set
Alpha Billionaire Club Boxed Set: 11-Book Boxed Set

Bad Boy Billionaire: A Billionaire Steamy Romance
Billionaire: A Box Set Book Series
Billionaire BBW Romance
From Agony To Ecstasy: A Billionaire Romance Boxed Set
Bad Boy Alphas Boxed Set
Heart Of The Billionaire
BWWM Billionaire: A Billionaire Romance Series
The Billionaire's Surrogate
The Billionaire's Virgin Surrogate
BDSM: The Billionaire Dom's Submissive Surrogate
Anatomy Class
Billionaire Daddy
The Billionaire's Secret Baby
Saved By The CEO: A Steamy Billionaire Romance
Billionaire Love Story

The Billionaire's Wish

Braden Davenport was on cloud nine. Even now, as he pulled off his helmet, he felt great. He was on a streak and this was going to be his best season yet. He brushed his hand through his jet black hair and smiled at the people around him. It was nice having fans. They were the only constant in his life, always there to cheer him on. The problem was, they didn't really know him.

That's not to say that it isn't great doing what you love for a living. He was able to buy his first house at the age of 23, and at 29, he owned three. He liked to have a nice place to stay whenever he was in his favorite places. Racing was a dangerous sport, but it was in his blood, a part of him. Being here in Austin for the MotoGP race had been a fluke, but a happy one. He was a last minute add in and he was happy he said yes.

He would always rather be racing than home alone or out with some nameless girl that didn't know him very well. For now, he was home in Texas, at least for the next two months. It was the place where this all began and he was happy to be there. He loved the dry air and the open grounds in the hill country, and the city life in Austin. His next race was in Vegas and he was happy for the break. The win today would put enough money in the bank that he could live off forever, but it was never enough. Having lived such a hard life growing up, he liked the better, secure, lifestyle he had now.

He basically lived his life in an orphanage. He never knew his father, who left his mother soon after he was born. His mother was heartbroken and soon became an addict. He still remembered what it was like finding her there when he was 7. She made the wrong person mad, and they gave her some bad stuff. He found her unresponsive, lying on the living room floor. They didn't have a phone, but fortunately he was able to run to a neighbor and they called the police for him. He still carried around the guilt because he couldn't save her.

He eventually left the orphanage and made a few friends. He had a difficult time trusting people, getting close to anyone.

He got his first job at the thrift store in town. He learned the hard way that life was about making the right choices or you end up with nothing. Over time, he managed to secure a room, and that's when he met Gerald and Abbie Smith. Older, they were frequent shoppers where he worked, and they always amused him. At 80, Gerald was a big bear of a man. Abbie was a tiny little thing at 77. Abbie would tell Braden he looked too thin, and Gerald would pull him aside and talk cars with him, something he always loved. After a year or so, they invited him to dinner. At 19, he still seemed like a kid to Abbie. She was always fussing over him and making sure he actually ate when he came over.

Gerald was the person who taught Braden to race. He owned many bikes, he was a collector of sorts, and the moment Braden rode one, his life changed. He maneuvered them like a pro. After some help from Gerald's contacts, he quickly became successful and was able to secure himself a lucrative future in racing. When Braden was 21, Gerald passed away, and Abbie followed a year later. He moved in to help her after Gerald's passing, and held her hand when she died.

That was seven years ago now, and he could still remember it like it was yesterday. He shook his head, remembering, and smiled. He made sure his bike was always in tip top shape, and made frequent visits to his trusted mechanic and best friend, Mike's house. They met in his early years of racing, and had been friends ever since.

The most important thing that Gerald taught Braden was that the bike is your money and the only way you can ride it safely is if you have a hand in what goes on with it. The bike was his family, and he protected it as such. He finally set off for the hour drive to Marble Falls, where Mike lived.

Mike was always a party guy. One girl to the next and one disaster away from an addiction. What he did have was a nice house, and a serious garage behind it. It was the one thing he always took care of. His mother would come over once a month and clean up for him. As he pulled into the parking lot of the townhouses, Braden noticed the changes. The place next door was vacant the last time he was there, and he wondered if Mike even knew that someone had moved in.

He was taking the next few weeks to run off with his newest girlfriend and had given Braden the key so that he could drop some things off, and pick up some things for the bike. He noticed her the moment he pulled up. He watched amused as a woman was desperately trying to get her key to work in her door knob.

"Damn it."

She was angry and she was beautiful. She finally kicked the door and turned to go to her car. She stopped when she saw him watching her. She gave him a half smile before pushing her hair back and squaring her shoulder.

"I'm not usually so easily flustered. My key broke off in the door... now I am rambling sorry... so yeah, I should go." She turned to go again and he finally said something.

"I can probably get that out of there if you want me to try." He crossed his arms as she gave him a half smile.

"That would be... well... yes, please." She smiled at him again and he went to the truck.

Chloe closed her eyes and took a deep breath. She was standing here rambling like an idiot. It always happened when she met a guy, especially an attractive one. Attractive didn't even begin to describe this one. He was, by far, the most attractive guy she had seen in a long time. He had black hair and dark eyes and just enough stubble on his face to give him that mysterious look. She never even kissed a guy like that and she never would. It certainly didn't hurt to watch him though. He was all muscle, and it was obvious he worked out. She blushed as he came back towards her, hopefully he hadn't seen her looking him over like that.

He smiled as he worked on the door. She was looking him over and it made him smile. The fact that she blushed when he looked at her made him like her even more. He finally broke the broken key out and he turned to look at her again. It was her eyes that struck him first. Deep blue and full of life, they contrasted the abundance of red flowing hair. She was a big girl, he liked that about her. She had curves in all of the right placed and he wanted to touch every single one of them. He glanced at her hand and didn't see a ring, which was a good first step. He handed her the broken pieces of the key, and when his eyes met hers, he saw her blush again.

"It should be fine now, I had to put some lube in it." He gave her a half smile.

"What... oh thanks." She gathered the pieces up and headed towards the door. "Thanks again..."

"Braden... my name is Braden." He held his hand out to her and she shook it.

"I'm Chloe, nice to meet you."

"Perhaps I can get you to have dinner with me sometime, Chloe?" He watched the myriad of emotions cross her face.

"Sure, that sounds like fun." She turned to head back in again and he smiled.

"Chloe, can I get your number?"

"Oh, sorry." She wrote it down and turned to go again.

She was a flighty one, but that was part of the excitement for him. He watched her go inside and he left, heading for his place in the hills. She was timid, something he would remedy. Even now he thought about her curves and how they would feel under his fingers. He rarely ever lost at this and he didn't intend to start now.

Chloe shut the door with a thud. That was very sweet of him, offering to have dinner with him. It was typical of some guys, nicer ones anyway, to offer to take the big girl out. She didn't need to get paraded around and everyone's opinion of him go up because he did her a favor. Still, he seemed genuine. She made her way into the house and took a good long look at herself in the mirror. She had been working hard to lose weight, to be in better shape. She was down 20 pounds but she still hated the way she looked. Aside from her friends and her little brother, she was alone. In some ways it suited her. She'd had one serious relationship and that left her ready to just put the idea of love and romance behind her for good.

After, she made her way into her room to throw on pajamas and spent the rest of the afternoon cleaning until Charlie got out of school. At 12, he was more than a handful of energy. In a week, he would be gone with friends on vacation, and she would really be alone all summer. He had been living with her a year and a half now, but some days it seemed like only yesterday that he had moved in. She was 22 and ready to tackle the world when she got the call. Her parents and her little brother were in an accident.

Like most people, she didn't think anything could happen to her. She rushed to the hospital, but her parents were both gone, leaving Charlie, with her. It was a rough start, but they were good now. She'd be lying if she said she didn't get lonely sometimes though. He kept her busy, one activity to another. Motherhood at her age was not part of her plan, but she was lucky they had each other. That thought brought her back to Braden. She wondered if he had a family. He seemed like a nice guy.

She never had an opportunity to meet her neighbor. As far as she knew the little lady that came in and out on occasion was the only one who visited that house at all. She sighed, she had rambled on and on about nothing, he must have thought her a complete idiot. Finally, she sat down to calculate how to pull off everything this month.

She was a local teacher, well she was a substitute. She was still in school part-time but she was determined to finish. Most of the time she worked enough days to just barely pay the bills, but having a 12 year old with numerous after school activities put a dent in things. Not to mention the rent on this place was out outrageous. Since her parents were renting as well, their place was too much for her to take on.

They were always like the traveling circus, always moving and changing. Chloe didn't want that for her little brother. She lived that life and he needed stability. She would simply have to cut out some things, but first she would have to find what those things were.

Braden walked into his house, well Gerald's and Abbie's house. They left it for him in the will. No children of their own, they took him in and loved him as if he were theirs. He didn't live here, it didn't feel like he should, and to be honest, he didn't want to take over. He liked being able to walk in and see their things as they left it. It gave him a sense of peace. Deep down, he knew it wasn't healthy, he should sell it, but for now he couldn't let go.

He checked on things here and then headed to the place he lived in the hills. He called ahead the week before so that it could be opened up and aired out. He hadn't been here in months and knowing it would be ready was one of the many luxuries he enjoyed. He had a house manager and a housekeeper, both trustworthy friends, and he compensated them well for the work they did for him.

Once he was there, he made his way inside and he poured himself a drink, leisurely making his way to the large windows overlooking the city. He wanted her. The thought crossed his mind and he smiled. Chloe, there was something about her that struck a nerve, and he wanted to figure it out. He thought at first it had been her coy and shy personality, but he had played that game before and knew that wasn't it.

There was a depth to her, and he wanted to know more. Women were always around, throwing themselves at him and offering him their charms. It came with the business... and the money. It was rare he felt connected to someone who didn't know about either of those things. She felt the connection too, but she simply dismissed it, and he wanted to know why. He suddenly smiled as an idea came to mind. She had no clue who he was or the money he made. Even in her wildest dream, would she ever guess that he was a billionaire. He pulled out his phone and called Mike.

Braden pulled up to Mike's townhouse once more with a renewed spirit. Mike had given him the green light at least for the next few weeks. That would be plenty of time to figure Chloe out. He glanced over at her place before heading inside. Much like his penthouse, the place hadn't been lived in in months. Everything shined and gleamed. "Thank you Mrs. Anderson." He said under his breath.

She was a sweet woman, often quiet and reserved, but she could clean the hell out of this bachelor pad. He decided there was no time like the present to start pursuing his curvy neighbor. He made his way over to her door. It wasn't late, so he gave it a knock. She opened the door in a flurry, and as soon as she saw him, she looked shocked.

"Braden hello." She smiled at him and he felt the heat rising in him. Her hair was pulled up on top of her head and she was wearing a t-shirt and sweats. Casual and damn near the sexiest thing he had ever seen.

"Hello Chloe, thought I'd see if you were up for a chat? It's just that I've been out of town and it's hard to get resettled." He gave her a smile and gauged her reaction.

She was just a little intimidated. She assumed he would move on and let her be, but here he was, in his tight jeans and arms that looked ready to rip out of his shirt. She gulped slightly, what was wrong with her? She usually had more control over herself than this. She gave him a half smile.

"I wish I could. It's just that my little brother is here and is sleeping." There, that should put him off.

"Oh, I see. Maybe we could sit on the deck?" He shoved his hands in his pockets and she mechanically nodded a yes. He smiled at her again and she moved to let him in.

She must be completely out of her mind. What was she doing? She didn't even know him that well and she just let him walk right into her house. He could be a crazy person or something. She sighed.

"I'm not a killer or anything, if that's what you're worried about." They had made it to the sliding door and he leaned in behind her, whispering it in her ear.

She felt the heat of his breath on her ear and shivered. It had been a long time, very long, and she was just sensitive that's all. They moved out to the deck, and as she shut the door and turned towards him, he was directly in front of her.

"Are you married Chloe?" He leaned towards her as he said it, propping his arm against the sliding door beside her head.

"You're very forward aren't you?" "No, I'm not, said Braden, are you?" She ducked through his arm and made her way over to the wrought iron chairs on the deck. It was dark out there. Having forgotten the deck lights were blown, she silently cursed. She turned around again, and this time he walked over to the rail. She joined him there, waiting and suddenly he turned towards her.

"No, I'm not." He put an arm on either side of her and rested against the railing. As he did so he leaned into her breathing in the scent of jasmine.

She was lost in that moment, He was inches away from her and her only thought was that he must be really desperate to be here with her. More than anything else, she didn't want to look like a fool, it's happened before and she didn't want to go through that again. She dipped below his arm and faced the trees again. She could hear his chuckle, and she frowned.

"You are something else Chloe, you know I want to kiss you, but you keep running, why?"

She looked at him, surprised by his admission. "Why do you want to kiss me? I'm sure you have plenty of other women to kiss, besides, I don't even know you, Braden."

"What better way to get to know me, Chloe." He stood and gave her a smile.

There was something about the way he said it that left her wondering if he was serious or simply out of his mind. She shook her head and turned back around.

"Don't be ridiculous Braden."

She said it simply and he realized she meant it. He frowned as he thought about it. Maybe she wasn't attracted to him. There was only one way to find out. He slid over to the right and grasped her hand in his and pulled her towards him. He saw the look of surprise on her face as he put his hand against the back of her head, pulling her into his arms as his mouth crushed hers.

She was on fire and he did nothing but add fuel to it. She felt his mouth nip at her lips and then dive deeper. She opened her mouth to him, unconsciously meeting his kiss eagerly. As their tongues danced, she felt the fire inside begin to build and grow. It had been so long, and he was very good. She felt his hands then start to move. First, slowly he ran them down her back and over the curve of her hip, pulling her even closer to him. She felt his mouth slowly leave her lips and trail down her neck and he nipped her collarbone. He moved his hands up her hips and his mouth found her again. The kiss was passionate and full of promise. She felt his hand slip under her shirt and she panicked, pushing him away.

Braden stood frozen, what the hell was wrong with him. He planned on sweet talking... maybe steal a kiss, but this... He ran his hand through his hair and walked to the deck to calm himself. One thing was for sure. She wanted him just as badly as he wanted her, she couldn't deny that now. He looked over at her, she was stone-faced and looked almost sad. He frowned, that was not what he expected to happen, but why would it make her sad?

"Chloe, I'm sorry." I didn't mean to get so carried away." She looked down and then back up at him, a smile now sitting on her face.

"I understand. Like you said, you haven't been home in months. I'm sure you're just tired." She moved to walk back to the door leading to the house. She whispered to herself "Plus it's dark out here, I'm sure that helps."

"Helps with what?" He was beside her, he was like a cat the way he moved.

"Nothing sorry, just rambling as always. I should get to bed, I have to be at work early." She smiled at him, but he knew something was wrong here.

"Sure, I understand." He turned to go and then spun back to look at her. "I like kissing you, Chloe. I won't lie about it, and in fact, I want much more than that. I wanted you to know I plan on trying to make sure you know that regularly." He walked down the front steps whistling. She stayed there until she heard his door shut. She leaned her back against the door to try and calm her racing heart.

The days went by quickly, they would often pass each other in the front yards or as they came home. Both of them caught up in work. He consistently asked her to come over for dinner, but she always had reason to say no. He never made any other move to kiss her or otherwise, and she relaxed more around him. They spent two different afternoons sitting out front talking about life, where each time she was sure they had an audience at all times. One afternoon she opened up more than she planned.

"So, Charlie?" Braden asked as Charlie was throwing a ball with a friend in the parking lot.

"My parents were killed in an accident, he was with them, but survived. That was almost two years ago now." She watched Charlie playing. "He is a good boy though."

"That has to be hard on you, suddenly having a 12 year old." Braden watched the expressions changing on her face.

"It took some adjusting, for all of us." She took a sip of water from her glass.

"Why aren't you married?" He asked it very matter of factly, but with a deeper tone to his voice. She turned to look at him.

"I almost was once, actually."

He sat up at her admission. So she had loved someone, being close to them. "You know you have to tell me now Chloe?"

"No, I don't Braden." She stood up, brushing off her skirt as she did and headed into her house. He stood and followed.

She noticed him standing in the doorway. "Really Braden, following me into my own home? Even for you that's a bit much." She started folding the towels on the table in the kitchen. He didn't say anything, but methodically started helping. She paused to look at him and he simply grinned at her. She rolled her eyes.

When they were done, he finally spoke. "Why don't you want to talk about it?"

She put her right hand on her hip. "Because it doesn't matter Braden, that's why." As she turned to go he grabbed her forearm and pulled her to him.

"It does matter Chloe, it certainly is part of why you are the way you are."

"What the hell does that mean "the way I am"?" She felt the sting then. She was different. Why did people always feel the need to point it out to her?

"Wait a minute Chloe what do you think I am talking about here?" He took another step closer, never letting go of her arm.

"Let me go Braden." Her eyes glittered dangerously.

"Not until you tell me."

"Fine." She yanked her arm free. "I was engaged, he seemed to accept me." She gave him a glance. "He was always sweet and kind and then when my parents died, he never made it to the funeral. He apologized, and I was stupid enough to believe him. When Charlie moved in, he tried to force me to send him away to a boarding school of some kind.

He said this was not the future he planned and that Charlie was not his problem. So I refused, and he slept with my friend. I caught them in my friend's house. The worst part was, it had been going on for a long time. She was one of those model-thin blondes. I should have known better." She looked over at him finally and he was in shock. He moved towards her again and she stepped back.

"I'm sorry that happened to you Chloe, he was an ass."

"Thanks."

Her voice was clipped and short now. He knew she was reliving it and it was his fault. He looked at her, she was sad and hurting and it had left something scarred in her. He felt that same feeling when he was put in that home. Like no one understood him or cared to. He didn't want that for her, for her to feel that way. He reached out and grabbed her again and pulled her to him. They stayed that way for a long time, just standing close with him pressed against her until Charlie came running in breaking the spell.

"Chloe, look what I found, a frog!" He happily made his way over to her and she shrieked backing up.

Charlie glanced at Braden, rolling his eyes. "Girls." Braden couldn't help but laugh at the scene before him.

"Well, I have to get going, Chloe. I expect to finish this conversation later." He ruffled his hand in Charlie's hair. "You be nice to your sister." He gave him a smile and he headed out. He had a tremendous amount of paperwork to sort through at his place.

The next week went by uneventfully. She would glance at his place when she went to work, subconsciously hoping to see him. He was a good friend of Charlie, and that was all. School would be out in two days. Finally, it was Saturday, and Charlie was leaving. She knew the Bakers were picking him up at 11 and she started helping him to move his things outside as they waited. He was smiling at her and she finally asked him why.

"You are gonna have a whole lot of time to spend with your new boyfriend next door when I am gone, Sis." He started laughing. She swatted at him.

"Charlie, that's not funny. Keep your voice down. He is not my boyfriend, he is our neighbor."

"Okay, so why is he always asking you out?" He looked up at her and started to laugh again.

"I don't know. Maybe he feels sorry for me because my little brother has such a big mouth." She pushed him as she made her way down the stairs.

"No, he likes you Chloe, I like girls at school... that's how he looks at you." He shrugged at her glare and went back to moving things.

"No, he doesn't, guys like him don't like girls... well like me. That's just the way the world is. It's up to younger guys like you to make the world better." She threw a pillow at him and he scrambled to catch it before it hit the ground. Finally, they noticed the Bakers coming up the side street, and after some time, he was loaded and leaving.

She waved at him, feeling a little sad at the prospect of spending so much time alone. Once it had been easy to fill her time, and now, she was like a mom, and without him, she wasn't sure what to do. She turned around and Braden was there watching her. She gave him a wave and headed back to her house.

He watched her go. It was the longest week of his life and all he wanted to do was touch her. Between issues with the races, complaints from other drivers about a leak, and his manager trying to set him up on random surprise dates at dinner time, he just wanted something normal. He wanted her. He heard what she said and it made sense to him now. "Guys like him and girls like her." She had no idea what he wanted, but he was going to tell her. He took long strides to her door and rang the bell. He felt the anticipation curling up. When she opened the door, he practically fell through it.

"Braden hello..." He cut her off, pulling her to him and covering her mouth with his. He bruised her lips with his attack and she felt her defenses slip away. She thought of nothing but him for a week.

They moved together in the living room and she leaned back on the couch as he pushed her down. She felt the length of him against her and it was perfect. His hands were everywhere and as he unbuttoned her shirt he felt her freeze.

"Look at me Chloe. I want you, all of you just as you are. Stop fighting me." She was still frozen and he knew he had to convince her. He pinned both of her arms above her head with his left arm as he moved his right hand over her curves. She was rounded and smooth, and he loved it. She was aware of every nerve ending in her body, as his hands reached around and under each breast, lifting her bra slightly so that the nipples were exposed. He cupped each globe lovingly until he reached the pert nipple that had hardened under his touch. He pulled and tugged on them, creating a deep ache deep down, soon covering each one in succession with his mouth.

Chloe was lost in the sensation. No one had ever taken time with her like this, ever. His hands were lighting her on fire with every movement.

She was all fire, just like he knew she would be. He was almost in pain with the need to rip off her clothes and bury himself inside her, but he wanted to go slow, wanted it to be good for her too. She was laid out on the couch, her hair, a red flaming swirl around her head and yet he could still tell she was nervous. He moved lower to make a final step in making her his.

Her eyes flew open as she felt him slide his hand under her and lift her off the bed as he loved her with his mouth. She couldn't move, couldn't do anything but feel the way he felt against her. She felt the tension fade away and the mounting pleasure begin to spiral out of control. Her legs were shaking as she climbed that ultimate peak to release. She let go of her resolve and fears and put her hands in his hair and let go.

He felt her release, and the way her legs were trembling made him ache for her more. He moved above her and watched her face as he moved to push inside her. She was tight, and it took more than one pushed to fully envelope himself within her. With a final push, he was exactly where he needed to be. He pushed her knees up and over his shoulders as his movements became more frantic, more demanding. Soon, he stood back from her, one hand holding each knee as he pounded into her relentlessly. He heard her moans, and knew she was sharing in the intensity. Her hips moved with his, and the explosion was powerful as he pushed into her one last time and release came.

They both lay there, trying to breathe and trying to make sense of what just happened. For Chloe, it was unlike anything she ever experienced. She looked up at him and he was smiling down at her. He leaned in and kissed her lightly before he stood up. She once again marveled at his chiseled body. He saw her glance and smiled at her. Hopefully she knew that he found her sexy and he enjoyed touching her. He made his way to the kitchen and Chloe quickly redressed. What had she done? She felt the blush rising up her face. He had seen her, all of her. No one ever had. She made her way into the bathroom and then followed him in the kitchen.

His phone rang and she turned to look at him and he frowned as he listened.

"Chloe, I have to go. I'm sorry, something came up."

"Sure it's fine go ahead." She felt the same fear from before, he would leave now.

"Chloe look at me." She did. "I will be back, I promise. " He kissed her quickly on the head and left.

To say he was worried was an understatement. The twenty minute drive took him 12. He pulled into his lot and stared up at the flaming mess. His penthouse was on fire and all he could do was watch. He found the house staff and was happy they were okay. The three of them watched as the fire department did their best.

The next few days Braden spent sifting through what had once been his home. His home hadn't been saved and very little else had either. He had to meet with the investigator today and then the adjuster. The police assumed this was an accident, but he wasn't as sure. He was staying at a nearby hotel, trying to hold it all together, but barely. He made sure the staff had rooms and that they were well taken care of. Most of his time was spent on the phone or on conference to various media networks and the racing team. He thought about Chloe, her smile and her sweetness. He missed her. Everything he put into proving he liked her the way she was vanished the night he left, and hadn't come back. He promised, and now she would never trust him again.

Chloe knew she was a fool. She spent that entire night waiting for him, as if she believed in his story, or that he would come back. She waited, and the joke was on her. Life had, inevitably gone back to normal. As a teacher, she threw herself back into the work of planning for the next school year. She found that by journaling a lot, she was able to keep her heart from hurting too much.

The reality was she cared about Braden and what he thought of her. The times they spent talking was a big part of that. He was a kind and sweet guy, despite his obvious fetish for big girls. It wasn't that he never came back that night. The fact was he had never come back at all, until yesterday. She hadn't actually seen him, just that his lights were on and music was playing inside. How he could just ignore her now was the brunt of the pain.

She wished for a moment that she had the strength to march over there and demand an answer, but it was better off left alone. She glanced at the clock and headed out to go grocery shopping. As she did, she heard the door open next door and she cringed. The last thing she wanted was a run in. She turned around and it was a woman, a very thin, very hot blonde woman. The blonde in question gave her a wave and she straightened her shoulders and left.

Braden had cancelled the rest of the afternoon and made the decision to try. He had to explain, and most importantly, he had to tell her the truth. He drove to her place and waited. He saw her car, he knew she was there, but for the first time since he was a child, he was scared. He was a nationally known bike racer and had been with more than a few women all over the world and this one woman had him questioning everything about himself. He felt the guilt like a punch in the stomach. Not just for leaving her like that, but for not telling her the truth about who he was. He finally got out of the car and went to the door.

She heard the knock and frantically made her way to the door. She found a solution to her financial woes and was moving in a roommate. To say the mess from what had once been storage was everywhere, would be putting it mildly. She climbed over the final boxes and pulled the door open. There he stood.

"What do you want Braden, I am really busy." She hoped the nonchalant way she talked to him would fool him.

"We need to talk Chloe, really talk." He sounded serious and she finally made eye contact. Still gorgeous, he looked rough. He looked tired and she knew something was wrong. She moved out of the way and he came inside.

He felt a sense of panic at the mess. "Are you moving?" He glanced around.

"No, I found a roommate. Nice guy, good job." She crossed her arms in front of her and waited. She would let him speak, but she wouldn't make it easy for him.

Braden felt a rush of anger. He would be damned if some "guy" was moving in here. "There are some things I need to tell you and explain. I need to know you will let me explain it all and then we will talk about this "guy" you think is moving in here."

He made his way to the living room and she followed. Her arms were crossed again and her eyes were flashing fire. Even now, he wanted her.

He turned the channel to ESPN and turned to look at her. "This is the best way I know how to explain."

She sat there stunned watching sports news, which she didn't even know existed. Some bike racer had a house that burned down and, wow, he was local. She suddenly felt sick. He was everywhere, pictures and stories and she knew. He turned it off.

"Oh my God Braden, are you ok?" She looked at him and touched his hand.

"I'm fine, my house is gone though. That's where I have been. That's why I didn't call."

"Why didn't you tell me you were famous? It would have made our fling that much more memorable for me." She gave him a half smile.

"Stop it Chloe, I don't look at you like that and I know you don't either. It's more than that and you damn well know it." She moved off the couch and towards the door. He caught her hand as she went by, standing up in the process. He kissed her forcefully, only letting go when they needed air. It was then he noticed her tears. He kissed her eyelids and wiped them away.

"Don't cry Chloe, please, I'm so sorry for everything." He pulled her into his arms and buried his head in her hair.

He kissed her face and then her mouth again. It started so simply, wanting to comfort each other, and soon they were lost in the moment. She pulled away from him and went up the stairs, and he followed. Once there, he took the lead, grabbing her hand and pulling her with him into the room. Their actions frantic now, they undressed each other. He turned her around to face away from him. She felt him unzip her dress and trail his fingers down her spine as the dress slipped to the floor. He reached around to cup her breasts, which overflowed in his hands. He pulled her back against him and she felt the hardness there.

"Don't ever question what you do to me Chloe, feel what you do."

She did just that, taking him into her hand and feeling the length of him. He pushed her over towards the bed and she climbed into it and he stopped her. She was half on and half off the bed when he moved behind her. He filled her suddenly and quickly, and she gasped at his entry. He moved his hand up to her hair, winding his fist in it and bracing himself as he plunged into her faster, and deeper. They moved together both seeking and searching for something. She was the first to reach her peak and she moaned out his name as she did so pushing him over the edge as well. He pulled her to him spooning behind her. She was his, and she always will be. Suddenly she stood.

"You should go Braden." She pulled her dress over her head and stood. He stood as well and she was once again reminded of how perfect he was.

"Chloe please."

"Braden this.... this was a mistake. You know it as well as I do."

"No, it's not a mistake, how can you even say that after what just happened?"

"We come from different worlds, Braden, you're... famous for God's sake and I am just some..."She trailed off. "You lied to me, Braden."

"I know, at first I just wanted you. I was driven by a need to be inside you, loving you. Then things changed."

"No, they didn't Braden... ...you should go... now."

He saw the firm set of her jaw and knew she was serious. He took one last look at her before he left. Chloe waited until she heard the front door shut and she locked it before crumbling to the floor and gave over to the tears.

Braden was not himself. His driving was awful and he couldn't connect with the course. He normally would love the flowing hills of Virginia, but he was officially not on a streak anymore. He angrily threw his helmet into the seat of the car and made his way to the crew. They all knew to avoid him when he was like this. Braden angry was a rare thing, but it usually had a quick turnaround. This time he was like this all day. He was angry, and worried. Chloe refused to respond to any messages he sent her and he missed her. She was so damn stubborn and it hurt that she didn't feel the same way.

Braden made his way into the hotel and caught a glimpse of himself in the mirror. He was dirty from the race, but he was changed now. He spent his entire adult life alone until this one woman came into it and now he was worried about someone else. He knew she had been struggling, in more ways than one. She shared her situation with him, told him her secrets, and he lied to her. He knew she was hurting, but couldn't she see how he felt? He frowned. How did he feel exactly? He got into the shower to wash away everything from the long day. He had to do something, and soon.

He met up with Mike for dinner that evening who put it all in perspective for him.

"You're in love with that chubby girl back home aren't you?" Braden stood and towered over him.

"Don't ever say that about her again, do you understand me?"

"Whoa, whoa buddy calm down. I didn't mean anything negative about it. I am just telling you man, you got it bad. The whole damn crew is afraid of you the way you're tearing things up all the time. Not to mention you lost your streak, you need to see her and make it right. Either let her go or marry the girl."

Braden sat back in his chair and thought about what he said. Marry her? The thought gave him a start of panic, but the idea of coming home to her, all the time was one he could love. He ran his hand through his hair. He hoped she and Charile were okay, if only she would answer his damn calls. He suddenly had an idea, one that might make her call him after all. He pitched his idea to Mike, who chuckled and started to make the call.

Chloe was frustrated. The roommate was an ass and he left his things all over her house. More importantly, he was indifferent to Charlie. Treating him like a bug in his way all of the time. Last night was the final straw. He came home drunk and groped her, and she was finished with it. She took a deep breath before knocking on his door. She had to do it repeatedly before he finally yelled something and stumbled to open it.

"What Chloe?" He moaned as she pushed the door open wider.

"You have to move, Josh. I can't have this kind of environment for Charlie."

"You can't just kick me out, Chloe. I have rights. Besides, you like it when I touch you, don't even try to lie." He took a step towards her and grabbed her again. This time she pushed at him and scratched his face. He gave her one blow to the face and she staggered backwards. She rushed to the living room calling for Charlie and the two of them made their way out to her car.

Mrs. Anderson watched the little car pull away with a shake of her head. That was a bad man in there, she saw her holding her face when they left. She pulled out her phone to call Mikey and tell him the plan couldn't work now. After Mike hung up the phone, it took him a minute to turn around. He knew once he told Braden, he would lose it. There was nothing he could do but to tell him.

"Well, what did she say?" Braden was eager to hear Chloe was ok.

"Seems like she is gone man, I mean she had a couple bags and she and Charlie left."

"What the hell do you mean they left?"

"Sit down man I'll tell you everything."

Braden did, only because he knew he wouldn't get any information otherwise.

Twenty minutes later, Braden called the airline and booked a flight to Texas. The sonofabitch was going to pay and he would be the one to do it. Mike tagged along, mainly because he didn't want Braden to end up in jail. They took the direct flight and Braden was full of tension and ready to fight the entire time. Finally on the ground, they picked up a rental car and made their way into the city. He was practically out of the car before it even stopped. He made his way to her house and when the door opened, he let the first punch fly.

Mike glanced down at the man on the floor. The guy didn't even have a chance. Braden knocked him out with two hits. Braden made his way upstairs and checked to make sure she had yet to come back. He wasn't sure where she would go, she had a few friends, but no one she spoke about enough to give him any clear direction to head in. He walked back over to Mike's and sat in the chair by the window so he could watch and wait. He glanced up at Mike.

"Give me your phone."

"Why?"

"Just trust me, I'll give it right back."

He took the phone from Mike and sent a text to her from his number. He visibly relaxed when he got a response. It was wrong, but it had to work. She would be furious, but he would at least get to look at her and make sure she was ok.

Chloe was concerned. The message said that she needed to come home right away. She wasn't even sure who sent her the message, but she had to find out what was going on. She dropped Charlie off at a friend's house and made her way home quickly. She had so much to figure out and she was exhausted. She glanced at herself in the mirror. It had only been a number of hours, but her right eye was purple and bruised.

She couldn't go back in there. He was horrible. What had ever possessed her to let him move in in the first place? Money, always money. She wanted to keep Charlie in one place with his friends, something she never had, and this is what happened. She pulled into her parking lot and got out of the car. She would wait out here. She couldn't go in there alone ever again. It was then that the door next door opened and she saw him.

It was only a couple of months, but he was perfect. He took a few long strides to get to her and before she could say a word, he wrapped himself around her and picked her up. He literally picked her up. She heard him whisper her name and she closed her eyes against the emotional overflow she felt inside her. Why was he here? She pulled away and he stood back looking her over. When he looked at her face, he swore.

"That asshole." He started walking towards her place and she went after him.

"Braden wait." She went behind him and they made it to the door. She grabbed his arm. Suddenly there was another man there. He pulled Braden away.

"Calm down man." Braden turned towards her as the police pulled up out front.

"Oh no, Braden the police?" She walked towards the car again. She felt his hand on her arm.

"Yes, the police Chloe. Look at your face and what he did to you." She tentatively touched her face with her fingertips. She saw the rage fill his face again and she touched him. "I'm fine Braden, really."

He watched her go speak to the police and he glanced at the front door as it slowly opened. Josh came staggering out and Mike once again grabbed Braden by the arm, preventing him from going to jail. The police made their way over to Josh and cuffed him. After they were gone, Braden turned to face her.

"We need to talk Chloe, now." He went inside and she soon followed, but not before Chloe saw the blond from before walking hand in hand with Mike. So she was never with Braden. Somehow that helped to make her feel a little better. At a wave from the two of them, she made her way inside where Braden was waiting.

"Braden, nothing has changed. I love that you came here to help me, I do, but we are still so different. Everything we do is..." She stopped as he kissed her. She closed her eyes, even if they couldn't be together, she could enjoy the way it felt when he kissed her, even just for another moment. She relaxed in his arms and he felt it. He pulled her even closer to him and ran his hands over her curves.

She was everything, and he wanted all of her. The kiss intensified and he undid the back of her dress pulling it to the floor. She was lost in him, his touch and felt the coolness of the air against her skin. She trusted him unlike she had ever trusted anyone else. He pulled her into the living room never stopping the kisses he trailed down her neck. When they made it there, she stopped him. She could be herself with him, for the moment. She walked around him and shed the rest of her clothes. She walked to the couch and laid back on it, fully unclothed and waiting. He watched her, his mouth hungry to touch her, but reveling in the way she was with him now.

She was no longer concerned about if he was attracted to her, or if he wanted her. She believed in him and how much he wanted to touch her. He finally moved towards her, gently moving his mouth down her chest, stopping to kiss and run his tongue over each crested peak. He buried his face in her breasts pulling on them and kissing every inch of them. She had her hands in his hair now pulling his head back up to kiss her deeply. He moved his hands along her curves and she arched up to meet them.

She moaned at the sensation and was aching for him with a need deep down. This is how he wanted her, how he needed her to be with him. He moved his fingers over her, working to a fevered state and he watched the expression on her face as she became more demanding of release. He wanted to give her more and he slid down, burying his face in her and tasting her.

He felt her hands in his hair as she grinded into him and finally he felt her reach that ultimate peak and he knew it was time. He raised above her, his excitement evident and she stood to touch him. Sliding her hands down his body over his chest and further until with a swift intake of breath, she held him in her hands. She slid to the floor, and when he saw her look up at him, it was almost too much. He pulled her up to him and kissed her deeply before pushing her to the couch again.

He mounted her swiftly, pushing into her depths. He reached the full hilt of himself and stopped. He wanted to just feel her surrounding him like this. He looked up at her face. She was flushed from her climax and eager for more, but he wanted to watch the expressions as he moved her. He moved slowly now stretching her to her limits and testing himself, his ability to prolong the inevitable.

He felt her hands on his chest as he looked down at her and he watched her curvy body move with his. He wanted her, always. He pulled out and slammed back into with a force that shook them both to the core. It had never been this good, this satisfying. The need was far too great and they both were aching to reach that final release. He moved faster now, steadily grinding into her and she was almost whimpering, and calling for him. He loved her like this, with abandon.

He increased his speed and was both grinding and pounding into her at the same time. It was good, too good. She called his name as her body moved on its own. She was no longer in charge of it and she felt the orgasm start low until it shuddered through her entire body, leaving her spent and breathless. Her explosion rocked him to the core and he couldn't hold back any longer. He slid his hands under her and lifted her off the bed slightly as he plunged into her again and again until he shared in her release. He buried himself inside her as far as he could. He wanted her to know he had given it all to her.

They lay there holding on to each other. Both afraid to speak, afraid to break the beauty of what they had shared. He knew she would run from him now, but he wouldn't let her. He was in love with her and he couldn't imagine life without her in it. She was the first to move, raising her head to look at him.

"Braden." She whispered and he gently kissed her lips. He held her that way, the two looking at each other waiting for the other to say something else. She was what he had been missing his entire life, she was family.

She raised up, suddenly self-conscious of her nakedness. He knew the person she was in the throes of passion was not who she was every day. It was a part of her she shared with only him, and he loved her all the more for it. He pulled her dress from the floor and helped her into it. He noticed she relaxed some and glanced at him sheepishly as she did it.

"Chloe, before you say anything, I need you to know something." He moved the strands of hair that had fallen into her face as she moved. She waited and looked up at him.

"I am in love with you." I know you don't know how this will work, but I know you have feelings for me too. I know you worry about everything, from yourself, to Charlie and money, and this house."

"Braden" she started, but he held up a hand to her...

"I'm not finished. The last few months have been the worst kind of hell for me. I found my mother dead on my living room floor when I was twelve, and aside from a loving couple who gave me a family for three years, I have been alone my whole life. I didn't even know what I was missing until you and Charlie. I love you. Chloe. I want you with me... you and Charlie. I have more money than I can ever spend and I want to share everything with you."

"Braden... I love you too." He relaxed with her words and pulled her closer to him. She was worried about life with Braden, what she never considered was how awful life would be without him. She smiled up at him and asked.

"Will you miss all the models and thin girls? Can I really satisfy you, Braden?

"Chloe, what we have is better than anything I have ever done in my whole life. You are sexy and gorgeous, and ALL I want is you." She smiled and a giggle escaped.

"What's so funny?"

"Charlie said you liked me even before any of this. Now I have to tell him he was right."

"I love you Chloe."

He kissed her again, and for the first time in her life, she believed it.

******

Second Chances

Brooke felt an immediate attraction to charismatic Sean the moment she first saw him at her best friend, Lisa's wedding. Although he was there with a date, Brooke couldn't help but stare at him.

Sean was stunningly handsome and sensual, and he had the most dazzling smile she'd ever seen. When Lisa returned from her honeymoon, she called Brooke and asked her what she thought about Sean.

"I thought he was gorgeous! Too bad he was with a date," Brooke said.

"She's not his girlfriend, and in fact, he seems to be interested in you," Lisa explained.

"You have my permission to give him my phone number," Brooke told Lisa.

"I already did," Lisa slyly replied.

When Sean finally called her, Brooke was jubilant, but she was so nervous that she couldn't think of a thing to say. She felt that their conversation was strained and awkward at first, but as it progressed, the couple's banter flowed freely and effortlessly.

Brooke learned that Sean was a wealthy investment banker who grew up only minutes away from her hometown.

"I'm sure that we know some of the same people," Sean said.

"Where did you go to high school," Brooke asked.

"Central, how about you?"

"Riverwoods," she replied.

The couple continued on with their small talk for what seemed like an eternity to Brooke, but after a while, Sean finally asked her out.

"What are you doing Saturday night?"

"I don't have plans yet," Brooke said.

Sean asked, "Have you ever been to that new restaurant on Mayfair Street yet?"

"Not yet, but I've been wanting to check it out for the longest time. I've heard that they have the best pub food around and that it has live entertainment on the weekends," Brooke replied.

Brooke didn't want to say anything to Sean, but her ex-boyfriend, Levi was the restaurant's manager.

She and Levi had broken up about a year ago after she found out that he was cheating on her with one of the waitresses he worked with.

Brooke was devastated by the break-up, and was convinced that she would never find love again.

"I'll pick you up at 7," Sean told Brooke.

"Great! I'm looking forward to seeing you."

While Brooke really didn't want to bump into her ex-boyfriend at the restaurant, she hoped that he would see her with Sean.

Levi wasn't the jealous type, but Brooke hoped that if he saw her with another guy, he might regret leaving her.

She recently heard that he and his waitress girlfriend were no longer together, and as far as Brooke knew, he was single once again.

Levi worked long hours at the restaurant and didn't have a lot of time for a social life.

When Sean arrived to pick her up, Brooke was dazzled by his rugged good looks. He was impeccably dressed and smelled delicious. She shamelessly stared at his perfectly toned body, and was starting to get excited at the thought of his touch.

"You look absolutely gorgeous," Sean told Brooke.

"Thank you. You don't look so bad, yourself!"

As the couple drove into the restaurant's parking lot, Brooke starting feeling anxious. What would she do if she saw Levi?

She thought about telling Sean that her ex-boyfriend was the manager, but decided against it, at least for now.

The restaurant was dark and cozy, which gave Brooke a sense of peaceful comfort. Even if Levi was working, she didn't think that he could possible see her, unless he walked up to her table.

Brooke finally started to relax, knowing that she wouldn't have to encounter an uncomfortable meeting with her ex-boyfriend.

The conversation between she and Sean was flowing nicely until he asked her about her past relationships.

"How long did your last relationship last?"

"About two years," Brooke replied.

"What happened, if you don't mind me asking?"

"Things just didn't work out between us, and we decided to go our separate ways."

Sean continued to press Brooke for answers about her relationship with Levi. Feeling uncomfortable by his intrusive questions, Brooke finally told him that she didn't want to talk about it anymore. Embarrassed by his boldness, Sean apologized.

After only a couple of hours, Brooke determined that Sean would make a good boyfriend.

She liked the fact that he was considerate of her feelings, had the same job for ten years, was close to his family, and had tons of friends.

While Brooke didn't enjoy talking about her past relationships, Sean had no problem doing so.

"My last relationship lasted for about five years, and even though we were in love, we both knew that it wouldn't last."

Sean further explained, "She was quite a bit older than I was and wasn't interested in having a family, which is something that I've always dreamed of."

He also commented that her family wasn't too fond of him because he wasn't established in his career yet.

From the side of her eye, Brooke saw someone resembling Levi. Her initial reaction was to quickly leave the restaurant, but after thinking about it, she decided to stay.

The person who looked like Levi was stopping at each table conversing with the customers. As it turned out, it was him.

Brooke's heart was literally beating out of her chest because Levi, the restaurant manager, was making his way to her and Sean's table.

"Oh my God, here he comes," Brooke said to herself.

Sean sensed that something was wrong, and asked Brooke what it was. At first, she didn't want to volunteer any information about Levi, but she knew that she had to.

"That guy over there, the restaurant manager, is my ex-boyfriend, Levi."

"Do you want to leave?" he asked.

"No, it's okay. I don't care if he sees me."

Before she knew it, Levi was standing at their table and asked, "Hi guys, is everything alright?

At first, Levi didn't notice that it was Brooke sitting at the table because he was looking at Sean when he greeted them.

As soon as he discovered it was her, he exclaimed, "Brooke, it's good to see you again!"

"Nice to see you too, Levi."

Brooke introduced Levi to Sean, and she could tell that they both felt uncomfortable when they shook hands.

Sean as was classy as ever during the introduction and he even engaged Levi in a conversation about the restaurant.

"This is such a great place. How long have you been working here?"

Levi answered, "I really enjoy it here. I've been with the restaurant for about three years."

He further added, "management is great and my co-workers are cool."

For some reason, Brooke was starting to get annoyed at how well the two guys were getting along.

After a few more minutes of small talk, Levi excused himself so that he could get back to work.

Before he left the table, however, he slipped a note into Brooke's purse, which was hanging off the back of her chair.

She didn't discover the note until the next morning when she was looking for some gum.

The note read: "Brooke, you took my breath away when I saw you tonight. After seeing you, I realized that I made a terrible mistake in letting you go. I know that you've moved on with your life, and I'm really happy for you, but sad at the same time."

Levi went on to say, "I am so sorry for hurting you and for turning your life upside down. If you could find it in your heart to forgive me, I'd be forever grateful. Please, Brooke, I'm begging for another chance. I've been constantly thinking about you for months, and I can't get you out of my mind. I feel powerless and helpless without you in my life. I'm in agony. Please call me. I love you, Brooke."

Brooke was stunned. Even in her wildest dream, she would have never guessed that Levi was still in love with her.

In fact, she assumed that she was simply a distant memory in his mind.

While she was flattered to learn that he still had strong feelings for her, she had no desire to reconnect with him.

Brooke finally told Sean about what happened between her and Levi and how he ruthlessly cheated on her with one of the waitresses he works with.

Sean seemed to sympathize with Levi and even went so far as to say, "well you guys weren't engaged or anything, so I really don't see a problem with it." This comment infuriated Brooke and made her reconsider her relationship with Sean.

While it was true that Brooke and Levi weren't engaged, they had a mutually exclusive relationship with an understanding that neither one of them would see other people.

After Sean's snarky comment, Brooke's entire impression of him changed for the worst.

This wasn't the only rude comment he made either. He also mentioned that he really didn't blame Levi for cheating on her because the temptation of being surrounded by so many beautiful cocktail waitresses would make any man stray.

Brooke couldn't believe what she was hearing, and she vowed that if Sean made one more snotty remark, she was going to stop seeing him.

In fact, the better Brooke got to know him, the more appealing Levi became.

While Levi did cheat on her, he always treated with her with the utmost respect and kindness throughout the duration of their relationship. She even feels partially responsible for their break up.

Brooke always pressured Levi into getting a better paying job and furthering his education.

She also demanded all of his time. Levi worked long hours, and he sometimes didn't get home until after midnight.

Brooke didn't care. She would often demand that he come over after work, even if it was late. Levi always complied, and never gave her a hard time about it.

This doesn't justify his cheating, but Brooke was now starting to realize that she may have driven him right into the arms of another women. One who was understanding, patient and not so demanding. Brooke craved his attention all the time and he felt smothered by it.

One of Brooke's co-workers told her that Levi's relationship with the cocktail waitress was staring to heat up again. She thought they broke up, but maybe not.

Brooke found this disturbing, especially since he recently professed his love for her through his letter.

Sean's behavior toward Brooke was starting to turn her off more and more. He always wanted to talk about her relationship with Levi, and even started pressuring her into revealing the most intimate details of their sex life.

Sean often asked, "Did you enjoy having sex with him?"

He further inquired, "Who was better in bed, Levi or me?"

Brooke replied, "You're being so intrusive and I resent all the questions." She also told him, "I'm starting to think that we should take a break from each other.

We used to be so happy and always had fun together. Now, there's always conflict."

"The reason there's so much conflict is because you don't want to share anything with me.

When I ask you for details about your relationship with Levi, I expect you to be forthcoming. You're so secretive about everything. I don't understand it," Sean remarked.

Brooke's responded, "I'm hesitant to talk about my former relationships because it's really none of your business. I don't ask you about the intimate details of your past relationships."

Sean was starting to fall in love with Brooke, but he didn't know how to tell her.

After all, they've only been dating for a short time, and he didn't want to come on too strong.

He knew that his prying would be a turn-off, but for some reason, he couldn't help it.

He didn't want to lose Brooke by being too possessive because he considered her his "dream girl."

The couple eventually decided to take a break from one another, and stopped dating for about a month.

During this time, Brooke re-evaluated her feelings for Levi. His note made her feel special, and deep down, she knew that he loved her.

The question was, however, did she still love him?

While she often thought about Levi, Brooke was staring to miss Sean.

She wondered if he felt the same way, so one night, after having a few drinks with some friends, she decided to call him.

"Remember me?" she coyly asked.

"I thought I'd never hear from you again," Sean answered.

"I really miss you, and came to realize just how much I care for you," Brooke said. "Can we meet for dinner next week to talk."

"Next week isn't good for me because I'm going to New York to visit my parents," Sean answered.

Brooke's heart sank. She was now convinced that Sean was no longer interested in her.

"How about Friday of next week?" he asked.

Excited, Brooke responded, "That sounds great, Sean. I can't wait to see you."

Brooke was anticipating her date with Sean and she hoped that they would be able to patch things up between them.

Even though he started acting like a jerk at the end, Brooke knew that he had a good heart, and that he genuinely cared about her.

When Sean picked her up, Brooke could barely catch her breath. He looked amazingly handsome and sexy.

They hugged for what seemed like an eternity, and being with him felt natural and right to Brooke.

The restaurant was romantic and the talk was sweet. By the time they got back to Brooke's house, they could hardly keep their hands off one another.

"Would you like to come in for a cup of coffee?" Brooke asked.

"I would love to."

They sat on the couch and starting kissing. Sean gently put his hands on Brooke's blouse. "I know I said I wanted to take things slow, but I'm not so sure now, so just go for it," she said.

He quickly ripped the blouse from her toned body and it fell to the floor.

His eager lips kissed her neck, while her hands unbuttoned his shirt, removing it from the waistband of his pants.

Brooke started out slowly, but then decided to bust open his shirt in the same manner in which Sean busted opened her blouse.

Her quivering hands found their way down his muscular chest, while he hungrily continued to kiss her.

Brooke arched her back, moaning each time he kissed her.

His strong hands rubbed her back, as he slowly took off her bra. Her ample breasts pressed firmly against his waiting chest.

Her hands unzipped his pants and she quickly removed them. Sean's hands went to his underwear while Brooke tugged on them to get them off.

He kissed her breasts while she eyed his ample erection. She was getting more and more excited with every glance, and when he undid the zipper on her dress, she was consumed with desire.

His hands went to her panties, looping his slender fingers through them, gently pulling them off her body.

Before Brooke had time to anticipate Sean's next move, she felt him pick her up, laying her down on the bed.

Their lips finally met, his eager tongue darting inside her mouth. As their tongues intertwined, his hands massaged her ample breasts, savoring the softness of her supple skin.

As Sean was ready to make love to Brooke, he hesitated. "Damn it, I don't have a condom," pulling back in disappointment.

She pulled him even closer. "Don't worry, I'm on the pill," she soothed, as they kissed and he penetrated her.

"It feels so good" she softly said, arching her back, but never breaking away from his kiss. His thrusts are deliberate and intense, which forces her to lose contact with his lips. It felt like a dream.

While one of Brooke's arms was holding onto Sean, she tried to grasp onto anything she could to hold onto as her body bucked up against his, finally choosing the side of the nightstand.

He had a hunger that she never experienced before. "Damn...yes...yes" he groaned, holding her even tighter to his body.

She could feel him pulsating within her, "God, yes..." she cried. She sighed deeply, almost unable to move, while his rhythmic grinding came to a halt. "That was amazing," she whispered.

As Brooke was basking in the afterglow, she felt Sean's hands moving up her legs, gingerly caressing her.

She wasn't sure what he was going to do, but when she felt his finger gently penetrate her, she moaned, savoring his every move.

In addition to using his finger, he began using his tongue to tease her.

As his tongue glided in and out of her, she reached down and grabbed his head to pull him in even closer to her.

After the interlude was over, Brooke was surprised at her lack of emotion towards Sean.

In fact, during the entire lovemaking session, she was thinking about Levi. She knew that it wasn't fair to Sean, but she couldn't help how she felt.

Had Levi never left that note in her purse, she feels she would have been better off. All these months, she barely thought of Levi. She was moving on with her life and socializing more than ever.

"Sean, I enjoyed our time together, but I can't help but feel that we're not right for each other."

"What about last night," he questioned.

"Last night was great, but there was something missing," Brooke replied.

She further explained, "I don't know how to explain it. I feel as though I should have been into it more, but I wasn't."

"Were you thinking about that jerk, Levi while we were making love?" he asked.

"Sean, I don't want to lie to you. Ever since I saw Levi at the restaurant, I can't get him out of my mind. He and I shared years together, and it's hard to forget about him. I thought I was starting to get him out of my mind once and for all, but seeing him again sparked some old feelings inside me."

"Brooke, please give me a chance to make you happy. I know I can make you forget all about Levi. You're just confused because you saw him again after all those months. The feelings you have for him aren't love. You're just confused."

"Maybe you're right, Sean," Brooke said. She further remarked, "Thank you for being so patient with me. I guess I am confused."

Brooke ended up giving Sean another chance, but as the weeks went by, she still couldn't stop thinking about Levi. She knew that she wanted to call him to talk about a reconciliation.

As she dialed his number, Brooke was shaking. She was hoping that his voicemail would pick up so that she could leave a message. It didn't.

"Hello?"

"Hi Levi, it's Brooke."

Levi's voice cracked as though he were starting to cry.

"Hi baby, I miss you so much. We should still be together. I really screwed things up between us."

"What have you been up to, and how serious are you with that guy I saw you with at the restaurant?"

"We've been dating for a while, and while we're semi-serious, our relationship can't compare with the one we had," Brooke said.

"Does this mean that I have a chance?" Levi asked.

"A very good chance," she said.

Brooke and Levi decided to meet at a neighborhood coffee shop, and when they first saw each other, they hugged and cried.

They both commented on how being together felt so right, and that neither one of them had found true happiness since the break up.

The couple decided that they wanted to spend the rest of their lives together, but they would first have to break the news to their current partners.

Brooke knew that Sean would take it hard, but he was a strong enough person that he would bounce back quickly and get on with his life.

Levi's current girlfriend, on the other hand, might not take it so well. She had been pressuring him for an engagement ring because she wanted to settle down and have a family with him.

"Let's go away for the weekend," Levi suggested.

While Brooke normally would have jumped at the chance to have Levi all to herself for an entire weekend, she didn't feel right about it. She wanted to end things with Sean before taking Levi up on his offer.

It disturbed her that Levi would suggest going away together before ending it with his current girlfriend.

"You'll have to end your relationship before I'll go away with you."

Levi reasoned, "I'll have a talk with her when I get back."

It was right then and there that Brooke decided she didn't want anything more to do with Levi.

He planned on cheating on his girlfriend just like he cheated on her. This brought back so many negative memories, and she really sympathized with the other woman.

"I see that you haven't changed much. You don't have a moral compass," Brooke said.

"Come on, Brooke, give me a break. I've been under a lot of stress lately. The restaurant is crazy busy, and I've been working 80 hours a week."

Levi further explained, "All I ask is that you give me another week to end the relationship. You'll see, Brooke. I'll do right by you."

"I'm sorry Levi. This isn't going to work out." I can't be with someone who seems like a serial cheater. You cheated on me, and now you're scheming to cheat on her."

"Brooke, you don't understand," Levi argued.

"Unfortunately, Levi, I do."

"I'd never be able to trust you. How do you expect me to love you when I can't trust you?"

"Goodbye, Levi."

Surprisingly, Brooke wasn't too upset about how it all played out. She felt worse thinking about how she hurt Sean when she broke up with him.

She even wondered if Sean would take her back. She hated the dating scene, and always preferred to be in a relationship, even if it did have some ups and downs.

Brooke was looking forward to reconnecting with Sean. She had a feeling that he was thinking about her, and would welcome her back with open arms.

They were always so connected to each other, and they both assumed that they would end up getting married one day.

Brooke couldn't decide on whether to text Sean or to call him. She longed to hear his voice, and hoped he would feel the same.

She dialed his cell, but he didn't answer. She didn't leave a message, but instead, decided to call him on the home phone.

After the phone rang about three times, someone answered it.

"Hello?"

Brooke was confused, because the person who answered the phone was a woman. She must have dialed the wrong number.

"I'm sorry, I think I have the wrong number," Brooke said.

"Who were you trying to reach?" the woman asked.

"A friend of mine named Sean," Brooke replied.

"You have the right number. This is his wife. Who can I say is calling?"

"Never mind. I'm sorry to have bothered you."

Badly shaken, Brooke trembled as she disconnected the call. How could Sean have met someone and gotten himself married in such a short period of time?

She felt that her dreams were shattered. She lost two men that she loved to other women. Maybe it was time for a change of pace, she thought.

Brooke decided to pack up and move to Florida, where she had family. She took a job in retail until she could find something in her field. While her new life wasn't exciting by any stretch of the imagination, it was quiet and serene.

If she met someone, it would be great. If not, she wasn't going to stress out about it. As the week turned into months, Brooke started feeling depressed.

Her social life was almost non-existent, and her job bored her to tears. While she had family in Florida, they were much older than she was, and they lived hundreds of miles away.

On a whim, Brooke decided to enroll in a cooking class at the local park district. She always loved to cook, but never considered herself a gourmet. Not only would the class give her the opportunity to brush up on her culinary skills, but she also might meet some new friends.

Brooke had so much fun on the first night of the class. The people were outgoing and welcoming, and the group was very diverse. Although Brooke was happy to meet the women the class, she was more intrigued by the tall, handsome stockbroker who also signed up to learn how to cook.

"Hi, I'm Jack. What's your name?"

"Brooke. It's nice to meet you, Jack."

She couldn't believe her luck. Not only was she engaged in an activity that she enjoyed, but she also met a guy. While she never met Jack before, he looked so familiar. In fact, he looked a lot like Levi, much to her dismay.

During the fourth cooking class, Jack asked Brooke out for coffee. She eagerly said "yes," but was shocked to discover who he was.

"Have you always lived in Florida," Brooke asked.

"No, I actually just moved here to manage a restaurant. My brother, with whom I'm estranged from, used to manage it, but ran it into the ground. The restaurant is owned by our grandparents, and when they discovered that he had been fooling around with all the waitresses and stealing money from the business, they fired him and sort of disowned him."

Jack further explained, "My brother has since moved out of state, and from what I hear, he's managing another restaurant."

A chill ran down Brooke's spine. Right then and there, she knew that Jack was Levi's brother.

"What's your brother's name?"

"Levi," Jack replied.

Brooke didn't let on that she was in a relationship with Levi. If things between them were to get serious, she would tell him. But for now, she didn't see a reason to.

Both Brooke and Jack enjoyed each other's company so much that they decided to go out on a real date. One date led to another, and before she knew it, the couple was engaged.

Through the grapevine, both Sean and Levi got wind of Brooke's upcoming wedding. By this time, Sean was already divorced from his wife, and Levi had broken up with his girlfriend. They each sent Brooke congratulatory emails, professed their love for her and revealed that she was truly "the one who got away."

******

Unexpected Romance

The blaring alarm clock on the nightstand jolted Jennifer awake. Too groggy to function after a late night at the lab looking over patient case files, she clumsily banged her hand around until she found the annoying culprit and slammed her palm onto the snooze button. Even after years of being lectured that it was better to get up the first time the thing went off, she never could. Only after two snoozes would she allow her eyes to crack open. Not a good habit for a doctor. There were patients to see and research to perform. Who was she kidding? After banging snooze buttons for twenty years, this was one habit she would never break.

After eighteen more luxurious minutes in her cozy warm bed, Jennifer couldn't deny the fact anymore. She had to get up and get going. Waiting any longer and she wouldn't have time for her morning run. No morning run meant a cranky woman—a cranky doctor at that. Not that she enjoyed running but it was the only time she could clear her head completely in order to focus throughout the rest of the day. Caffeine could only help so much so running had become her go-to activity. As much as Jennifer despised the bitter cold of a February morning in the nation's capital, she threw back the covers to begin her day.

It would take at least a mile before the fog of exhaustion began to lift from her mind. The first mile was always the most torturous. After that though, Jennifer could run forever. Adrenaline finally pumping through her petite, 5' 2" frame, she could take on the world. This morning in particular she needed the respite.

Being a pediatric oncologist was her life's dream. That is, after Hannah, her best friend from elementary school suffered horribly and died from a brain tumor. It was the reason she became a doctor in the first place. No child should have to suffer like that, ever. And no parent should have to endure such a loss. But cancer was indiscriminate and unforgiving. Last night she suffered yet another battle with her childhood demon. A three year old child with lymphoma. Jennifer had been so sure her latest protocol would work. She had spent the rest of the night beating herself up for failing yet another patient, another distraught family. Sometimes her life's dream was actually her life's nightmare. This morning she welcomed the punishment of the frigid air filling her lungs as she near sprinted the remaining blocks from her small condominium on K Street to the National Mall. Her destination – the reflecting pond overlooking the Lincoln Memorial.

Once she reached the ice-speckled pond, she allowed herself a moment to rest and take in the beauty of the landscape. Still too early for the onslaught of commuters and tourists who flood the city daily. All was quiet except the occasional rumble of jets overhead as they were taking off from Reagan National. Whether from the freezing temperatures and wind assailing her eyes or from sorrow and frustration at her failure last night, tears ran down her freckled face. Jennifer didn't know what was worse. Losing the patient or the fact that after so many years she still had not toughened up enough to make that pain any less.

Not wishing to dwell on the matter anymore, Jennifer raced back home. Shutting out all thoughts and allowing her body to operate on autopilot. New day, new challenge! She wouldn't allow self-pity to stop her. After many battles lost, and a few won, her determination was greater than ever.

After a quick, scalding hot shower Jennifer towel-dried her short strawberry-blonde locks and made a beeline for the coffee pot. No breakfast. She couldn't remember the last time she actually ate breakfast. Probably before leaving home for college when her overbearing mom would force her to eat before she could leave for school, even if it meant she was late. Her shift didn't start until 10 AM so there was plenty of time to either tidy up her small, 640 square foot condo or aimlessly peruse the internet. Without a second thought, she plopped down in her oversized khaki arm chair with her laptop.

Not obsessed about politics and news like everyone else in this town, Jennifer decided on lighter fare. How long had it been since she'd been on Facebook? Probably since her high school reunion that had been organized via the website, forcing her to get an account. Surprised that she actually remembered her password, the site loaded. Wow! Fifty-two "Friend" requests?! Jennifer was surprised she knew that many people. The newsfeed was filled with funny pictures of cats and babies. Quickly scanning through all the miscellaneous vanities, she noticed a posting from one of her best friends from her days at the University of Colorado. It was a picture of her tall, slender, runway model friend Jacy Standish with her college beau Ethan Davis III. The posting showed the couple with Ethan on one knee and Jacy with the biggest smile ever. Yes, it was the couple's engagement announcement. "Well, it's about time!" Jennifer thought. They have only been together since forever, it seemed.

The posting was a few days old so thankfully Jennifer still had time to send them a congratulatory message. The announcement declared that the wedding was to be at the end of May in Cocoa Beach, Florida. The couple had been living there since Ethan graduated with an advanced degree in aeronautics and went to work with NASA. In lieu of formal invitations, since there was nothing formal about Jacy nor Ethan, the Facebook announcement was also serving as the wedding invitation. Any friends and family that could make it should reply to the posting. "Well, that's certainly a modern approach." Jennifer grinned as she knew it was typical of the couple to be that nonchalant about their own wedding.

After clicking the "Like" icon and commenting a quick "Congrats!" Jennifer noticed she had messages. There were five messages from Jacy. The bride-to-be was curious why Jennifer never answered her home phone and why didn't she have voicemail. The next message scolded her for not keeping in touch and providing her friends current contact information as she was desperate to talk to her sorority big sister and best friend. Another message instructed Jennifer to call her STAT because she had a very important question to ask her. Looking at the clock, she realized it probably wasn't too early to call so she picked up her phone to dial the number listed in the last message.

A groggy Ethan answered the phone but was more than delighted to disturb his soon-to-be wife who was already awake and had just returned from walking the dogs. Jacy's squeal of delight nearly ruptured Jennifer's eardrum. After letting Jacy run on for several minutes about the upcoming wedding and lecturing her friend on her lack of manners for not staying in touch, she excitedly asked the burning question... "Jennifer, will you be my maid of honor?" This was followed by more declarations that she HAD to be her maid of honor and she was NOT taking no for an answer. Typical Jacy.

Promising to check her schedule and to get back to her later that day, Jennifer ended the call hoping she would not have to disappoint Jacy but uneasy with the thought of attending a wedding. Her own personal life was, well lacking the personal part. She was not a big socialite, even though the Chief of Pediatric Oncology enjoyed forcing her to attend fund raisers to benefit the hospital whenever he saw fit. Social settings were just not her thing.

Jennifer noticed another message in her inbox. This time from a blast from the past male friend, also from college, Lorenzo Esposito. Now what could he want? They hadn't spoken to each other since graduation. Despite being close friends in those days, she realized she didn't even know what his post-grad plans entailed. Although they had hung out quite often, going to sporting events together and the occasional party, Jennifer had been too busy trying to get into medical school and Lorenzo chasing skirts around campus for anything more to ever develop between them. Friends had teased that they should stop trying to fool everyone because they obviously belonged together.

She and Lorenzo would just laugh it off with a mischievous wink at each other. Never had anything other than a platonic "just friends" relationship ever entered their minds.

Curious what Lorenzo had to say after so many years, Jennifer clicked on the message. It was short and sweet. The usual, "Hi, how are you? I'm fine. Long time, no see." He had heard about the wedding and Ethan had asked him to be the best man but he was lacking a date to the event. Even though they had not kept in touch he was hopeful she would save him from having to RSVP as "1". He went on to explain that he was uncomfortable taking a "date" since weddings were seen as either the kiss of death for a relationship or as getting in line to be the next sucker down the aisle. He could do without the hassle either way. Lorenzo went on to note that he noticed her scant profile on Facebook as showing she was still unattached so he was pleading once again for her help, just like the good ole days in college. He needed a no-frills, no-strings attached wedding date and was hoping she would agree. "Wow! What a romantic?!" she thought sarcastically. He ended the message with his contact information if she was interested in helping him out.

Signing out of Facebook without responding, Jennifer took up her now tepid coffee and thought back to the outgoing, charismatic, undeniably handsome man Lorenzo had been in college. Tall, dark, and handsome didn't come close to describing him then. For a moment she allowed herself to imagine what he might look like now years later. She had to admit, the picture in her head was nice...very nice, indeed. Throughout college Lorenzo had always attracted the ladies, in droves. At one point their group of friends had taken to calling him "Casanova" because of his love'em and leave'em attitude.

After college the gang had all gone their separate ways. Jennifer had been horrible about keeping in contact with anyone. However, she did remotely recall Jacy mentioning that Lorenzo had married a woman he met at his first job after graduation. Jennifer had been surprised the mighty Casanova had fallen so soon. It must not have worked out if he was hitting her up for a wedding date.

While heading out the door to the hospital, she promised herself to clear her schedule at work so she could attend her friend's wedding. Besides she had not taken time off from the hospital in all her years working there. Not even for holidays to go visit her folks in Denver. She was due some R&R and this was the perfect excuse. As soon as she cleared the time off with her boss, she would contact Lorenzo.

After making her rounds at the hospital later that day, Jennifer sought out the Chief of Pediatric Oncology, Jacob Mallory, to discuss her "vacation". She found him where she expected to find him...on the phone in his office attempting to drum up more money for the department from a donor. He motioned for her to take a seat while he wrapped up the call. Jacob was not just the chief of her department but she also considered him a friend. He was of average height but built like a linebacker. His physique was always displayed at its best in Armani or other designer suits with his dark blonde hair cut short and always clean-shaven. Outside of the hospital environment he could easily be mistaken for one of the bigwigs up on Capitol Hill. He was equally suited to the political life. After all, wining and dining for cash from the elites was his specialty.

Ending his call, he turned his piercing aqua blue eyes on her with a charming grin meant to make her melt but somehow she never felt the impact of his bedroom eyes. They briefly discussed her current case load and results of some tests she was running on a new patient. She hoped the prescribed protocol would work since the cancer seemed to be caught in the early stages. The results were still being validated but Jennifer was optimistic. After a few minutes she got up the courage to voice her request. Looking somewhat shocked, but pleasantly surprised, Jacob reassured her that vacation time was much overdue for the workaholic doctor. However, he added that he would be delighted to go with her. Jennifer knew that was a danger area. She had attended some hospital fundraising functions with Jacob and knew he was attracted to her but she had no desire to complicate their relationship. Declining with the excuse of spending time with old friends, she thanked him as she rose from the uncomfortable office armchair to attend to the remainder of her day.

Later that evening, Jennifer returned to her snug condo with a large brown paper bag filled with several containers from the corner Chinese restaurant. Not realizing until much too late that she had not eaten at all during the day, she was ravenous by the time she headed home. Not even bothering to transfer the food from the take-out containers to a plate, she dove into the combination fried rice first. After satiating her hunger and fixing a cup of jasmine tea, she sat back down in her favorite armchair and pulled her computer onto her lap.

First, she notified Jacy that she would indeed attend the wedding and be her maid of honor. Luckily, Jacy was so laid back that she allowed Jennifer to pick out her own dress, as long as it was lavender in color. "Terrific," she thought, "purple does nothing for my Irish freckled complexion." Next, she composed a short message to Lorenzo stating she would attend the wedding and would also appreciate a "no strings" date. They could arrange to meet up once they both got to Cocoa Beach. Before signing off the computer, Jennifer booked her flight, a rental car, and her suite at the resort where Jacy and Ethan would be married.

Following a hot shower and veg'ing out to some reality television show for an hour, Jennifer retired for the night. The wedding had given her something else to think about aside from her young patients awaiting a miracle cure. Jennifer briefly entertained the hope that tonight her sleep would not be interrupted by nightmares. Maybe there would instead be images of warm sands and the sound of relaxing waves and a tall, dark, and handsome man.

The wedding approached quickly and Jennifer left a muggy Washington, DC over Memorial Day weekend for the hot and humid climate of the Central Atlantic Florida coast. In the last few months she had managed to grow her strawberry-blonde locks out just past her shoulders, and had even gone in for a professional mani-pedi a couple hours before her flight. A friend from the hospital had taken her shopping for a dress suitable for the occasion. Despite the lavender not being her best shade, Jennifer was surprised she was actually happy with the selection. She was not happy with the 2 inch high heels they had selected though. She hadn't worn heels since medical school graduation. However, they were necessary as her dress was long and her legs were short.

After a short plane ride and an even shorter drive from Orlando to Cocoa Beach, Jennifer arrived at The Cocoa Sands Resort and Spa shortly before the wedding rehearsal. If she was lucky, she would have a chance to stroll on the beach before meeting everyone in the ballroom. Luck was not to be had as Jacy spotted her friend in the lobby and rushed over to hug and greet her. Jacy was still the same as in college. Super model gorgeous with long legs and shining long blonde hair. She took charge of the situation and sent the bell hop to the room with Jennifer's luggage while she dragged the weary traveler to the outdoor bar area where everyone else had already congregated.

Seeing some familiar faces and some not-so familiar faces, Jennifer was handed a drink while making introductions and greeting old friends. Not all of the old gang was here, it seemed. She would have to ask Jacy about that later since she was being reprimanded for being the last to arrive by Jacy's mom. Through the crowd, at the other end of the bar, sat a very familiar handsome face – Lorenzo. The groom immediately piped up that he was just glad his buddy's date had finally shown up because it was a shame for such a man to be all alone. "Oh no!" Jennifer thought. She had heard this line of discussion before quite a number of times during college. Anytime Lorenzo had been girlfriend-free for more than five minutes, Ethan and Jacy had pushed them to get together. Maybe agreeing to this wedding date was a mistake.

There wasn't a lot of time for conversation as the wedding planner came out to the bar to escort the wedding party into the ballroom for rehearsal. Jennifer could tell this lady ran a tight ship and thrived on the stress of producing the perfect wedding for her clients. Considering how laid back Jacy and Ethan were about such thing, they had waited several years to tie the knot officially after all, Jennifer was surprised in their pick for a wedding planner. Guess it was better for someone else to stress about the wedding because the bride and groom weren't going to do so. As they were walking back into the hotel, Jennifer felt a soft touch on her elbow. Turning around she gazed up at her incredibly tall, incredibly attractive, wedding date. Lorenzo always had the most amazing smile and it was in full force as he linked their arms together to usher her into the ballroom. The warmth from his touch was reassuring and familiar as he had escorted her to a dozen or more functions in college. "Yes," she thought, "This was a good idea." Wordlessly they entered the ballroom with the rest of the party and took their respective places.

The rehearsal, thankfully, was short and sweet. Jennifer was ravenous since once again she had forgotten to eat that day. A full seven course meal awaited everyone in the main banquet hall of the resort. The tables were littered with place cards with centerpieces of fragrant candles and rose petals. She was looking forward to the meal and getting reacquainted with Lorenzo, as well as other long lost friends from the good ole days. Engaged in conversation with Janice, another former college friend who had always been known as the "mother" of the group, Jennifer felt someone staring at her. Looking around she discovered two of the darkest, most gorgeous chocolate brown eyes gazing at her from across the room. Lorenzo had already found their designated places and had her chair pulled out for her. Mumbling an excuse to Janice, Jennifer began to walk over to him realizing she was being way too self-conscious about herself as she neared him, with her head slightly bowed but looking up through her lush brown eye lashes shielding brilliant emerald green eyes. "Why am I so nervous?" she thought with some frustration.

The dinner was superb and the conversation flowed easily around the table full of college pals. Janice was married with a passel of kids, all under the age of eight which were at home in Pennsylvania with her husband. Kyle had his own architectural firm in Dallas and had just become engaged to his assistant Sarah. He assured everyone that they were invited to the nuptials next winter. Candace was a divorced nurse and single mom but was hoping her boyfriend of the last three years would finally pop the question. He responded with a flamboyant roll of his eyes. Everyone was in good health and good spirits. It truly was fantastic to be back with her group of friends. Until now Jennifer had not realized just how much she had missed them. Her world now consisted of work, work, and more work. No friends really outside of the hospital and definitely no boyfriend.

Lorenzo, however, remained quiet as everyone else discussed their lives since college and plans for the future. Jennifer didn't remember him being the quiet one. He was always the jovial, fun all the time, type of guy. He would offer a small smile or laugh as appropriate, but seemed to be staying outside the conversation instead of a part of it. His silence unnerved her but she didn't wish to ask unwanted questions but made a mental note to ask Jacy about the alteration in Lorenzo later.

With dinner over, the wedding party moved back to the outdoor bar area where they could enjoy the cool ocean breeze and their drinks. Not realizing just how tired she was, and there wasn't nearly enough food in her stomach to combat much more alcohol, Jennifer chose a lounge chair by the pool to relax in. At least she could kick off her strappy high heel sandals she had been in all day. Her feet were going to really hurt tomorrow. Jennifer had worn nothing but sneakers and crocs since graduating medical school. She was not cut out for heels, despite the need for added height, as she barely topped out at 5'2". Everyone else gathered around the pool deck, sipping mai tai's and other fruity umbrella drinks. Ethan started the group on something he called zombie brain shots. She didn't know what was in it but it looked disgusting. Jennifer declined. With that the party was in full swing. Good thing the wedding ceremony wasn't until late afternoon tomorrow as this particular group was going to need some hangover recovery time in the morning.

The party lasted well into the evening but most began to file away to their respective rooms shortly after midnight. Jennifer had nearly fallen asleep in her lounge chair. It wasn't until the last of the chattering died away that she noticed she was alone except for Lorenzo who had taken up a perch along the side of the pool, splashing his feet around. Throughout the after-dinner party, he had still remained quiet. This was not the man she remembered from college. The larger-than-life sexy, fun-loving Casanova. This made her sad and want to find out what was bothering her friend. Yes, they had been out of touch for many years. However, she found that she still cared about his well-being and had missed his presence in her life all this time. She got up from her lounge chair and walked over to the pool to sit down beside him. For several moments, they just sat there without saying a word.

Lorenzo was the first to break the awkward silence between them by remarking about being proud she had realized her dream of being a prominent pediatric doctor in a renowned hospital. It was a vague attempt at small talk. She thanked him and then they sat in silence for a while longer until Jennifer couldn't bare it anymore. Turning to him and looking up into his eyes, she saw sorrow reflected in their dark pools. There was an overwhelming desire to just hug him tightly as if he needed a shoulder to cry on. The urge was so strong that she did timidly reach up to stroke his cheek, which was prickly from a day or two old growth of beard. Instead of withdrawing from her as she feared, he placed his hand over hers and held it for what seemed many moments with his eyes closed. "La mia bella amica," he uttered softly.

After sitting a few more moments in silence, Lorenzo turned to Jennifer with that old familiar smile she was accustomed to seeing. "I'm so sorry for being such a poor date. It wasn't what I planned at all. I thought the wedding would be a good distraction for me and instead I've only been sad since arriving here. That's no way to treat such a beautiful lady," he said with sincerity. She could tell he was sad but didn't understand why.

Jennifer gazed up into his eyes and said softly, "I'll forgive you but you have to tell me why you are so sad. I was expecting this larger than life happy-go-lucky dude from my youth. Seeing you this way makes me sad and worried. This 'date' as you call it can only get better but you have to be straight with me."

With that he sighed and let the tale spill out. He had married several years ago to a wonderful woman, Lisa. They were happy and even happier when they became a family with the birth of their son Raphael. A spirited five year old that was a miniature version of himself with his wife's quirky sense of humor. Their happiness was cut short a couple years back when Lisa was killed in a horrific accident on I-66 coming home from work one day. She wasn't even supposed to be on the roads but had offered to deliver company documents to the Senate sub-planning committee chairman since he and his business partner were overwhelmed completing a project for another client.

Lorenzo continued his story about how he was struggling as a single dad. Business was fine but he worried about his son growing up without his mom. If he had to admit it, he was also lonely and missed his wife very much. He thought he'd brave it out for Ethan and Jacy by coming to the wedding but it was taking more of a toll on him than he had imagined. That was why he had sent her the Facebook message. He knew if anyone could see him through this weekend, it would be Jennifer. "Guess I should've been more upfront and explained all that beforehand. Quite frankly I never thought you'd say yes. Figured you had some hot shot doctor boyfriend to escort you here." With that last statement he actually conjured up a small teasing half-smile.

Jennifer continued to hold his hand and listen for hours as he told stories about his wife and his son. He took out his iPhone to show her a picture and the boy was indeed a copy of his handsome dad. Their conversation flowed to other topics such as her career and lack of a personal life, what they had been up to since college, and reminiscing about their time together in school. Before they realized it the sun was coming up over the ocean horizon and they were still seated on the pool deck with their feet dangling in the water.

As the hotel staff was starting about their day, Lorenzo and Jennifer went to their own rooms for much needed rest. Despite no sleep since the day before, her head was spinning with everything he had told her. After getting through all the sadness, they had reconnected during the course of the night. Felt like she had her friend back and with that thought she was able to close her eyes and sleep.

A few hours later a loud banging awoke her. She had overslept. It was Jacy with the brilliant smile of a happy bride. The two women exchanged stories as Jennifer jumped in the shower and got ready for the day. Thankfully, the wedding planner had arranged for someone to do their make-up and hair. All she had to do was make herself presentable. While waiting on her friend, Jacy took pleasure teasing Jennifer about her late night sojourn with Lorenzo. Jacy had always hoped the two would end up together, ever since their freshman days. They had thwarted every attempt by herself and Ethan to make the transition from friends to lovers. Secretly, Jacy wished that her wedding might light a fire in their direction but she kept that information to herself.

A few hours later, after a quick brunch, getting dolled up by the resort's spa staff, and getting the bride squeezed into her lacy, halter-top styled wedding gown, it was time. Jacy didn't seem nervous at all. She and Ethan had been together so long the wedding was just a formality. Jennifer, on the other hand, felt shaky as she proceeded down the carpeted aisle from the pool area to a spot on the beach where the groom and his handsome best man awaited. Traversing the terrain in high heels had been a bad idea after all. She nervously glanced up as she approached them and saw Lorenzo smiling at her with a gleam in his eyes. She gave him a quick wink and stepped aside for the bride's arrival, trying her best not to trip.

The wedding was short and simple. No frills but still sweet and romantic. Within minutes Jacy and Ethan were pronounced husband and wife, kissed, and everyone cheered. Jennifer glanced over to see how Lorenzo was handling the situation. She needn't have worried. He was all smiles and staring straight at her. Her stomach experienced an unfamiliar butterfly sensation, but she dismissed it in her mind as needing to eat something. "It couldn't be more than that," she thought.

The reception was held in the ballroom with French doors that opened out to the beach area. During dinner Lorenzo gave a sincere, yet hilarious toast to the bride and groom as he regaled the wedding guests with the story of how the two had met, had instantly despised each other, but within a week were caught making out in the chem lab. Everyone laughed, except Jacy's parents. It was her turn. Jennifer had forgotten she needed to make a toast so she tried to wing it. After stumbling around for the right words, she went with the traditional congratulatory message to the groom with best wishes for the bride. Then reversed herself saying "Knowing Jacy as well as I do, maybe the best wishes part belongs to the groom. Hope you have a big enough closet for all her shoes and that you don't live near an animal shelter since Jacy will bring home every single dog, cat, bird, mouse, whatever."

Music began shortly afterwards and the dance party ensued. Jacy and Ethan had always been big dancers and had dragged Jennifer and Lorenzo to all the clubs around campus. Jennifer was never comfortable in that environment, but Lorenzo always seemed to make it okay. Just like old times, he stayed by her side the entire night and didn't pull her out onto the dance floor until a Frank Sinatra ballad began to play. He didn't even ask. Just took her arm and led her out to dance. She recognized the strains of "The Way You Look Tonight". Lorenzo was the only person who understood her preference for Frank Sinatra over Nirvana. It had been a running joke that Jennifer had arrived at campus in a time capsule from the 1950s because she never liked the typical "alternative" music most co-eds did.

They danced closely. For some reason Jennifer couldn't find the courage to look up into his eyes. All she could focus on was the feel of his hand stroking the small of her back through the flimsy dress material as they danced and listening to the beat of his heart as she laid her head on his chest. If they were back in school they would be bantering back and forth about who was the better dancer or just joking around in general.

Too soon the song ended to be replaced by "The Chicken Dance". Hoping to escape, Jennifer pulled away to walk back to the sidelines but Lorenzo had other ideas. Yes, she was going to have to endure this most ridiculous wedding ritual. She was sure the "Electric Slide" would follow soon enough, but hoped they had seen fit to exclude "The Macarena". Before realizing it, it had been several upbeat dance numbers and she was still on the dance floor. Sweaty and thirsty, she motioned to Lorenzo that she was getting a drink. He followed closely behind as they grabbed a couple champagne flutes off a nearby waiter's tray and strolled outside for a breath of fresh air.

Removing her shoes on the sand, they walked out to the edge of the Atlantic Ocean. The sun was setting over the horizon. Jennifer plopped down on the sand to take in the beauty of the scene as she rarely saw the sunset anymore since she was always at the hospital or in the lab. Lorenzo joined her as they silently watched the glowing orange orb seemingly descend into the water. It was the first time in years that either of them had felt peaceful. This weekend had done wonders for them both, whether they realized it or not.

Unaware of the passage of time, the bride and groom came searching for them an hour later for the bouquet and garter throwing tradition. Jennifer always tried to make herself scarce during this particular portion of any wedding but decided to humor Jacy this once. Luckily, one of the groom's sisters was intent on being the next to get hitched and knocked everyone out of the way. Lorenzo stood stock still as Ethan threw the garter right at him and let the item fall to the floor where the pre-teen ring bearer grabbed it up. With all the wedding traditions complete, the bride and groom quickly made their exit so they could start the real celebrations in the honeymoon suite. The rest of the wedding party meandered around the ballroom for a while longer but started to disperse for their own rooms. Jennifer looked over at Lorenzo with a coy smile and motioned for him to follow her.

Earlier that day Jennifer had spotted a billiards room down the hall from the spa area. In college they had played pool against each other relentlessly. A few times they had partnered up to swindle money from unsuspecting underclassmen. With a wink, she began to rack up the balls and selected her cue stick. "How about a friendly wager? For old times' sake," she challenged.

Laughing, Lorenzo accepted her dare. After requesting a couple drinks from the bartender, he asked, "So what are we betting this time? It's not like I have a research paper I need your help on anymore and I don't think they will allow me on the plane with a case of scotch. What's it gonna be, little girl?"

"Alright there, jolly green giant," she teased back with the pet name she had given him freshman year, "We're both relatively successful people. We could actually bet real money this time."

With a frown, he replied, "No. No. That's no fun. Let's make it interesting. Whoever wins gets to make the other either tell a truth or take a dare." This proposal had potential but Jennifer was a little wary recalling past dares from him but decided to just go with it.

"You're on, big guy," she retorted with a smirk. Even though she hadn't played pool in years she was confidant it would come back to her. However, the strategy didn't work quite as she had planned. After thoroughly whipping his opponent, not once but three separate times, Jennifer admitted defeat and pleaded for mercy.

Appearing deep in thought Lorenzo issued his ultimatum. Truth or dare? Always uncomfortable with the truth category, she chose "dare". His dark eyes sparkled at the prospect as he contemplated his request. "Okay, I dare you to skinny dip in the pool or ocean right now."

Thankfully the alcohol that had flowed all night helped her find courage to do so but she was still not happy about it. After trying several times to convince Lorenzo to go "Best 5 out of 7 games", she resigned herself to her fate. Even the bartender snickered as she headed out to the door to the pool. After seeing that the pool was a bit too well lit for her liking, she chose the darker, more concealing ocean. Jennifer timidly approached the edge of the surf to test the water temperature before shedding any clothes. Being the Atlantic Ocean, it was chilly no matter what time of year.

Looking back to see Lorenzo standing smugly a few yards back, Jennifer instructed him to turn around and close his eyes. Despite it being nighttime, the moon was full and cast too much light on the beach for her liking. Grumbling under her breath that she should have known not to accept a dare from that man in particular, she tried the zipper at the back of the dress. It wouldn't budge. After a number of failed attempts she gave up and called for Lorenzo to help. The look on his face said that he was enjoying this a bit too much. He unhooked the clasp at the top, which she had completely forgotten about, and then slowly slid the zipper down to the small of her back. Her skin was chilled from the cool breeze coming off the ocean but where his fingers barely grazed her back as he worked the zipper almost seemed on fire.

She shook her head slightly to clear her head. "Must be the alcohol affecting me," she reasoned.

With the zipper situation remedied, Lorenzo retreated to his spot on the sand a few yards away. Being a gentleman, he turned away as she undressed. Still in her undies, Jennifer started to enter the water when she heard, "Skinny dipping means skin only, little girl," followed by a smug chuckle. Wincing at being caught trying to cheat, she shed the rest of her garments and plunged into the waves.

Resurfacing quickly she looked over to see Lorenzo doubled over laughing. Wishing to get out of the frigid water and avoid any ocean inhabitants, she tersely instructed him to get a towel or at least turn around while she put her clothes back on. He turned away still laughing. As she came onshore she couldn't find her undies. In her haste she had discarded them too close to the edge of the water and they had floated away with the tide. Reaching for her dress, Jennifer realized that due to being thoroughly drenched, she had difficulty getting it back on. After a few minutes struggling, Lorenzo had finally ceased laughing and questioned what was taking so long. Embarrassed she admitted the truth causing more laughter to erupt. After a few seconds, she started laughing too at the ridiculousness of a thirty-something year old doctor childishly taking a silly dare to strip off her clothes and run into the ocean. Her present predicament with the dress just highlighted the hilarity of the situation.

Finally regaining his composure, Lorenzo backed over to her so as not to see her clinging to the flimsy dress. He had left his suit jacket in the billiard room so he unbuttoned his dress shirt and handed it to her. Being so tall and Jennifer being so short, the shirt covered her almost to her knees. Playfully hitting him in the chest with the crumbled up dress, they made their way back to the hotel.

Luckily, due to the lateness of the hour, the lobby and hallways were relatively empty. Lorenzo escorted her back to her room. They were both still giggling when they arrived at her door. As she turned to open the door, Jennifer found herself wanting to invite him in for a drink but thought better of it. Instead she thanked him for a memorable "date" and gave him a quick kiss on cheek before retreating into her suite and closing the door behind her. She stood with her back against the door for several moments contemplating why she had gotten so nervous just now. It was just Lorenzo after all.

Jennifer practically snuck out of the hotel the next morning to leave for the airport. Not sure why she didn't want to run into anyone, particularly Lorenzo, she was packed and driving away almost before the resort starting serving breakfast. Apparently she wasn't the only one attempting to escape unnoticed. As she entered the airport lobby she spotted his tall, dark head of hair at the check-in counter. The silly, flirty looks the airline attendant was giving him made Jennifer roll her eyes. Lorenzo could always turn seemingly normal women into acting like gaga teenagers drooling over him. In college it had been entertaining to watch. Now, she was just annoyed.

Momentarily he turned around and caught her staring at him. Flashing that swoon-worthy smile he walked over on the pretense of helping with her luggage. "Hope you remembered my shirt when you packed this morning," he joked. They compared airline itineraries and discovered they were on the same flight to Reagan National. Appearing happy about the situation, Lorenzo proceeded through the line with her to the check-in counter where he requested a seat change for her so they could sit together in first class. The same attendant as before did not seem thrilled to fulfill his request. Jennifer stifled a giggle as the woman banged away on her computer terminal to make the switch.

They had plenty of time to stroll to the concourse as the flight wasn't for another two hours. Lorenzo suggested stopping for coffee and muffins. Jennifer agreed to the coffee. "Are you still not eating breakfast? No wonder you are so tiny," he remarked. Two tall vanilla lattes later, they were seated in the terminal with nothing to say. In silence they sipped their coffees and stared out the window waiting on their flight to arrive.

Finally, Lorenzo broke the silence by saying, "Listen. You know my situation and I know yours. Neither of us is looking for a relationship, but I really do miss your friendship. I was kind of hoping we could keep in touch more, especially now that we know we live in the same metro area. Also, we could help each other out of awkward situations, like going to weddings or events without the stress of someone thinking it was a real date." Jennifer nodded her head in agreement and looked up into his chocolate eyes. Having a sexy standby, go-to date was the perfect solution. She stuck her hand out to shake his to seal the agreement, but he leaned in and gave her a quick peck on the cheek.

The return flight went quickly as they discussed a myriad of topics. He spoke mostly about his son and his genetically-inherited love of soccer. She discussed her work at the hospital and how she wished she had more time for research since she felt a big breakthrough was just around the corner. Before they knew it, the fasten seatbelts sign lit up and the airplane descended. Having the window seat, Jennifer always enjoyed the arrival into this particular airport as it gave the illusion that the plane was about to crash into the Potomac River right before landing safely on the thin strip of land.

After retrieving their luggage, Jennifer made to give him a swift goodbye hug. Instead she found herself in a giant bear hug. Neither really wanted to let go. Saying goodbye, they headed their separate ways. Lorenzo to the parking garage to drive back to the DC suburb of Warrenton, VA. Jennifer to the Metro station to take the train into the District.

Jennifer's thoughts remained on Lorenzo the entire ride back to the station closest to her Georgetown condo. It was a long walk from there in the humid weather with the clouds overhead, threatening rain. She didn't notice though. Her mind ran over the events of the past couple days. Never in the last few years had she allowed herself to daydream.

She was just too busy for that. Nevertheless, as a spattering of rain drops began to fall Jennifer didn't even notice as she replayed the Sinatra song dance over and over in her mind. She blushed at the memory of her skinny dipping escapade. But the image that kept asserting itself was of Lorenzo smiling wickedly at her as they played pool. Her skin still felt the faint trace of where his fingers had brushed against her back unzipping her dress. Perhaps agreeing to be each other's go-to wedding date had not been the greatest idea.

Jennifer resumed her normal schedule and didn't hear from Lorenzo for a couple of weeks. Trying to justify her increased interest in Facebook, she lied to herself that she wasn't really just seeing if there were any messages from him. She was genuinely interested in everyone's pet pictures and what they had for dinner. Then one stormy evening as she was relaxing after a long day at the hospital with a cup of herbal tea and a bowl of sugary kids' cereal, her Facebook page finally indicated she had a message. Surprisingly, she could feel her heart beating faster in her chest when she saw that it was indeed from Lorenzo with an apology for not contacting her sooner. He indicated that he wasn't really comfortable communicating via social media and requested her number instead, or at least a viable email account. He included his full contact information in the message so she took out her cell phone and plugged in his information after sending a quick reply with her own information.

Later that night as she was just getting out of the shower the phone rang. No one ever called her except the hospital so she assumed it was the dreaded "There's a patient in distress" or worse call. Without glancing at the caller id, she answered and was delighted to hear the deep, husky voice of Lorenzo. Jennifer was surprised he called her so soon after she sent her contact information. Still wearing a towel and her hair dripping wet, she sat down on her bed to chat.

Hours later she was still wearing a towel with her hair dried naturally wavy and tousled. They had talked about everything and nothing, it seemed. When Jennifer happened to glance over at the clock she was shocked to see it was well past midnight. As she tried to say goodbye, Lorenzo surprised her again by stating there was a particular reason for his call. He needed a date. His son's teacher was getting married. His son really wanted to go to the wedding, but Lorenzo dreaded the matchmaking that would go on if he showed up without a female companion. Every one of Raphael's teachers and room moms seemed to make setting him up with any available female in the school district as their personal goal in life. He hated it! "Please, please, pretty please," he begged, "save me from this impending disaster!" Laughing at his predicament, she tried to play coy with her answer just to tease him. Ultimately showing pity, Jennifer agreed. She wrote down the date and time on her whiteboard in the kitchen and made a mental note to double check her schedule at work. Jokingly thanking her for saving his life, he said good night. Once she hung up the phone, doubt set in. Not only was she going to another wedding with him. She was also going there with his son. Jennifer wished she had thought of that before saying "yes".

As it turned out, she wasn't scheduled to work the day in question so no backing out that way. Her supervisor, Jacob, was somewhat taken aback when he later asked her to attend a hospital fundraising event at the Mayflower Hotel that same evening. Teasing her about finally getting a social life, he mildly suggested that he hoped she still had time for her research. The comment was completely uncalled for but had its intended effect by making Jennifer doubt herself. "Was it really necessary that she spend her time helping out an old friend, who quite frankly should be getting set up on dates in order to meet someone and provide a mother-figure for Raphael," she thought. "Perhaps it was selfish of her to want to spend time away from the hospital or anything benefitting the hospital when saving children's lives with her research was the most important thing in the world." After mulling it over, she had almost convinced herself to cancel with Lorenzo. However, when she tried to call him to tell him so, he sounded so excited and grateful she was going to be there with him that Jennifer didn't have the heart to turn him down.

Not having a car since living in DC, on the date of the teacher's wedding, she took the Metro to the subway station farthest west of the city. Lorenzo would pick her up there. To avoid walking the many blocks to the Metro station in painful high heels, she slipped her comfy sneakers on and packed the heels away in an oversized designer purse her mother had given her for Christmas. The vision of a petite woman in a pale green sundress and sneakers must have been amusing because Lorenzo starting chuckling as soon as he saw her emerge from the station. "Cut it out, meathead, or I'm turning around and getting back on that train," she threatened.

"Hey, Dad! You going to let her get away with calling you that?" said a robust little boy voice. Lorenzo was so tall she hadn't even seen the little boy behind him. He was a perfect miniature of his father with dark olive skin and jet black hair that was a little too long and kept falling over his large, almond-shaped eyes. He was dressed in a khaki pants, with a button-down shirt and even a clip on tie. The perfect little man, except for the dirt-smudged sneakers on his feet. "My kind of kid," she thought. She wondered how much Lorenzo had argued with the boy to get him in the dress clothes.

Lorenzo laughed and replied, "Yes, I will let it slip this once since she is a lady and we should always show them respect." With that he introduced his son and the little man reached out to shake her hand. Being a little Casanova himself, the boy adeptly turned her hand so he could bend over to kiss the top. Jennifer thanked him and complimented him on his attire and manners. He, in turn, commented on her brand of sneakers since apparently they were not the "in" brand of his generation. As the two continued to debate the finer aspects of various sneaker brands, Lorenzo escorted them back to the car.

To say Raphael was charming was indeed an understatement. He entertained Jennifer the entire ride to the church where the wedding was to take place. She was so captivated by him she forgot to change her shoes in the car. As she stepped out of Lorenzo's white Chevy SUV, he made a little "hmm hmm" noise. When she looked up at him oblivious to the problem, he started laughing. This time Raphael jumped in to scold his father for laughing at a lady. After thanking her little hero, she finally noticed the issue and started laughing herself. This seemed to confuse the boy. After his brave defense of the pretty lady, she was now laughing. When she sat back down in the car and pulled out her high heels to change he was even more shocked. How could one explain to a five year old boy that he could get away with wearing sneakers to a wedding but a lady could not? Raphael just rolled his eyes and said "Whatever".

As they walked arm in arm towards the church, Jennifer admired her escort out of the corner of her eye. Lorenzo looked dapper in a light grey suit and plum colored silk tie. His hair had grown longer since the wedding in Cocoa Beach and fell over his right eye hiding a small scar just below his eye brow. Jennifer recalled him explaining the scar to her one night. When he was ten years old, an opposing team player was angry at losing a game and in the last second of the game kicked the ball as hard as he could right at Lorenzo's face, splitting the skin above his eye. Just before walking into the church, she reached up to brush the hair away from his eyes and unconsciously allowed her finger to lightly trace the scar.

As soon as they entered Jennifer felt that all eyes were on them. At least all the females in the room were looking at Lorenzo and sizing her up. He may not realize it but she could tell some of those females weren't too happy to see another woman on his arm. Lorenzo, on the other hand, saw more than a few envious stares from the attending men. He knew he had a hottie on his arm and he enjoyed the satisfaction of knowing that this fetching beauty was with him. Just friends or not, he was still proud to be seen with Jennifer whether she was in sneakers, a formal dress, or just his shirt. The image of her wearing his shirt coming off the beach had haunted him ever since that night. Attempting to shake off the vision, as they were in a church and that could only lead to "un-churchly" thoughts, he moved to shake hands with some of the gentlemen in the foyer and to introduce his date.

They were ushered into the crowded sanctuary by an elderly gentlemen and took their places in a middle row. Luckily the ceremony started soon after their arrival as Jennifer was feeling awkward having so many people looking her over She knew they were evaluating in their minds if she was good enough for the handsome man next to her. Some, she noticed, frowned. Others gave a small grin of approval. However, there was more than one that gave her an outright evil look. The buxom blonde in the third row was obviously not happy with her presence. Sweet-natured Raphael kept leaning over to point out and whisper the names of everyone he knew. The blonde in question was the teacher's assistant in his class.

The ceremony was beautiful and much longer and formal than Jacy's wedding had been. Raphael was well-mannered and remained quiet and observant the entire time. Too bad the three preteens in the back row weren't so well-mannered. When the ceremony was over, they went back to the car to drive to the local country club for the reception. Raphael resumed his constant chatter with Jennifer. He pointed out his school and his team's soccer practice field. He described, in detail, his last game where he scored the winning goal against his arch rival Landon. The boy definitely had spunk and character. Jennifer already loved him and they had only been together for an hour or more.

The reception was held at an antebellum-looking house overlooking a pristine golf course. There were tennis courts adjacent to the building and a pool with colorful winding slides behind it. After dinner the children were taken to another room in the building where they could play arcade games or use the indoor basketball courts while the adults stayed in the banquet hall for dancing and drinks. Several people came over to introduce themselves, including the teacher/bride. One sweet middle-aged woman, who had already had a bit too much wine with dinner, commented that Raphael's dad had outdone himself with his date and that she shouldn't mind the other women there giving her jealous stares. Laughing, Jennifer agreed wholeheartedly. However, she was shocked when the blonde teacher assistant strutted over, and without acknowledging Jennifer's presence, asked Lorenzo to dance. He was stunned as well and indicated he already promised his date a dance. With that, he led Jennifer to the small dance floor as the music changed from some hip-hop number to a more subdued soft rock ballad. Trying not to giggle, Jennifer glanced over at the blonde woman who had stormed off.

The rest of the evening, Lorenzo and Jennifer kept mostly to themselves. Dancing when it was a slow tune and sitting out the club dance music. Raphael came bounding into the room again when he tired of the game room. Deciding it was time to leave, they again congratulated the bride and groom and made a beeline out the door. Once outside, Lorenzo issued a genuine sigh of relief it was over. Jennifer now understood why he had needed her tonight – to fend off the hordes of women wanting to throw themselves at him. "Must be a tough life," she thought as she started to giggle. Raphael just looked confused. He was so cute at that moment, Jennifer had to resist the urge to pinch his little cheeks. She was pretty sure he would not appreciate that.

The little boy seemed genuinely upset when they arrived back at the Metro station for Jennifer to catch her ride home. Looking into his sad face, so much like his father's, she promised it would not be the last time they would see each other. Surprising even herself, she asked him for a hug which he gladly provided. The look on Lorenzo's face as she shyly glanced up through her eye lashes, was a mixture of sadness and pride. Jennifer imagined he would give anything to have Raphael's mother here to give him hugs. Standing on tiptoe, as she had quickly reclaimed the sneakers when they had left the reception so was lacking the added height from the heels, she gave Lorenzo a quick kiss on the cheek while holding onto his hand so as not to topple from the effort. Being so tall, she was truly on the tips of her toes. He, in turn, held the tips of her fingers a little than necessary as if not wanting to let go. With a reassuring smile, Jennifer turned towards the Metro station to leave.

Lorenzo sent a thank you message to her via Facebook the next day with an emoticon of flowers. After that Jennifer didn't hear from him for over a week. She tried to convince herself she wasn't disappointed and refocused all her energies on her patients.

A new protocol she had designed was showing positive results for a couple of her younger patients in the earlier cancer stages. Unfortunately, it had been too little too late for one young boy in the more advanced stages of lymphoma. It had been an incredibly difficult day as she dealt with his loss. Jennifer kept chastising herself for not developing the protocol sooner so she could've saved him. Jacob, after seeing her distress, ordered her to take the rest of the day off. Several hours were spent running to rid herself of her demons. The ones that tormented her every time she lost a patient.

She heard her phone ringing as she approached the door to her condo. Unable to unlock the door fast enough, she missed the call. Checking caller id, she recognized Lorenzo's number. The voicemail indicator came on and she pushed the button to listen. He had just heard from their mutual friend Kyle in Dallas. His wedding date was set for the first week in December. The official invitations would be in the mail soon but he suggested booking the flight and hotel sooner rather than later. His fiancé had just discovered there was a convention of certified public accountants in the same hotel as the wedding. He ended by jokingly asking if she was up for yet another wedding.

Not in the mood to think happy thoughts that should always go along with weddings, Jennifer postponed calling him back until later that night. Despite trying to sound cheerful, Lorenzo sensed something was off. Changing his manner of voice from jovial to concerned, he asked what was wrong. She didn't mean to have a meltdown but was unable to say the words without her voice shaking and tears springing to her eyes again. She hadn't lost a patient in months and this time it really hit her hard. He listened sympathetically and tried say reassuring words of comfort. His heart ached for her as the agonizing pain in her voice was clearly evident.

Feeling exhausted from her emotional ordeal, Jennifer apologized for making him listen to her pathetic troubles. He assured her that it was no trouble and he was happy to be there for her anytime. Suddenly he asked her address. "Oh, great!" she thought. "Now he thinks he needs to send me a sympathy card or something." After giving him the information, Lorenzo did the strangest thing. He abruptly said he had to go but would contact her soon. Surprised by the change, she muttered a goodbye and hauled herself up off the sofa to get a much needed shower.

A couple of hours later her home phone rang with the tone indicating someone was buzzing her from the front entrance to her building. Alarmed, she asked who was there and was startled to hear Lorenzo's deep voice announcing himself. After hitting the button to unlock the door to the building, she ran to the bathroom and was dismayed at what she saw looking back at her in the mirror. Her eyes were puffy and her nose a bright shade of pink after all the crying she had done that day. "Oh no. I'm a total mess," she scolded herself. Splashing some cold water on her face didn't seem to help either. Too late. Lorenzo was already knocking on her door.

Taking a deep breath she opened the door. Without a word, Lorenzo reached out and drew her into an embrace. They moved inside the condo without breaking apart. As the door closed behind them, her tears started again. He held her as she sobbed. It wasn't until her body relaxed against his and her tears were spent that he gently pulled away just a little to look into her eyes. She saw his sympathy for what she was going through but she also saw something else. Almost as if it pained him to see her like this.

Realizing she must look a mess, Jennifer made to move away to get some tissues. Instead, Lorenzo tenderly stroked her cheek to wipe away a stray tear. His large hand cupped her face tenderly as he continued to gaze into her watery eyes. Not even realizing what she was doing, Jennifer leaned towards him and put her arms around his neck. Slowly, as if afraid to break away but also afraid to move closer, he tilted his head so they were eye to eye, nose to nose. Moments passed where Jennifer could only feel her heart thudding in her chest. Finally he closed the final distance and softly touched his lips to hers.

Tenderly at first and then with more urgency as long pent-up desire welled in them both, they kissed. His soft, sensual lips covering hers. As the kiss intensified his tongue parted her lips with a light stroke. The movement sent thrilling shivers through her body that left her hungry for more of him. Their tongues explored one another as if dancing to their own soft ballad. Deep inside her, Jennifer felt heat waves of passion surging throughout the body. From her very core to her limbs, long denied feelings bubbled up numbing her mind to anything else but the luscious feel of his body pressed against hers.

Lorenzo deftly guided them towards the oversized chair which was the first piece of furniture he could find. He settled her into the chair and knelt in front of her without breaking their connection. His hands caressed her face and neck as he deepened the kiss. Desperate to have him even closer her hands found the open collar on his shirt which she used to tug him closer to her. All thoughts had vacated her mind as soon as his lips had touched hers. There was nothing but sensation and the fire scorching through her veins.

Breathless, he pulled away to look into her blazing emerald eyes. There was a question in his eyes that remained unasked. Jennifer answered, without hesitation, as she pulled his head back towards hers. The intensity of their mutual need for each other was unable to be denied any longer. Had it always been there? Lorenzo gently scooped her up in his arms and moved them towards her bedroom.

Hours later, as the sun began to shine through her bedroom window, Jennifer stretched like a satiated cat as she ran her hand over Lorenzo's muscular sleeping form. The light streaming between the blinds only accentuated the perfection that was the man. Despite knowing him for years and seeing him in everything from a tuxedo to swim trunks, never would she have dared imagined him like this. Naked, in her bed, with his tousled hair covering his eyes as he continued to slumber. Jennifer reached up to move the hair away from his beautiful face so she could get a better look. Seeing him asleep it was hard to believe this angel was the same man that had taken her to such dizzying heights of ecstasy last night. She blushed at the memories.

Then realization struck. If he was here, who was with Raphael? How had she not thought of him before? She shook Lorenzo awake. He groggily sat up and reached for her as if to replay the events of last night, but she stopped him by the distraught look on her face. "Hey, I thought we got rid of that facial expression last night. What happened while I was asleep?" he asked.

She couldn't believe he didn't know. "Raphael. What about your son? Please tell me you didn't leave him alone just to come all this way to console me," she begged. With a huge sigh and laugh, he told her that the reason it had taken him so long to get here last night was because he packed up Raphael and sent him to a sleepover at a friend's house. Jennifer nearly collapsed back on the bed in relief. Of course he had taken care of his son first. Seeing her concern for the boy, Lorenzo smiled up at her and pulled her close. First he kissed her eyelids, then trailed light kisses down her face and neck before coming back to her mouth. They fell back on the bed together and spent the rest of the early morning enjoying each other.

A couple hours later, they had both showered and dressed. He needed to get back to coach his son's soccer game that afternoon. She had rounds to complete at the hospital and she was already late. As Lorenzo kissed her goodbye he asked her to come out to the game and spend time with him and Raphael for the weekend. Maybe she could even pack an overnight bag, he suggested. An offer like that was too good to refuse so she agreed to text him when she reached the Metro station closest to Warrenton. With a final longing kiss, they parted ways for the day. Both anticipating seeing each other again in just a few hours. Both exhilarated by their realized passion for each other and both nervous about where that left them as friends.

Jennifer found herself smiling like a silly lovesick girl as she made her rounds at the hospital. A couple nurses read the signs and were happy for the beautiful workaholic doctor. They commented, "It's about time that girl got a man!" Even the fretful parents of her patients picked up on her improved demeanor. This was a side to their child's doctor they had never witnessed. It was refreshing. The only person not happy about Jennifer's improved mood was Jacob. Although he had never officially made a move on her, he still thought of her as the one he would eventually captivate and marry. She had all the attributes of the perfect wife – gorgeous, highly intelligent, career-centric, and most importantly, she could charm the bigwigs in Washington out of their money for the hospital with just a bat of her eye lashes. Yes, Jennifer was his ideal candidate for the job of Mrs. Jacob Mallory. She, of course, was completely unaware of his plans.

As she finished with her files and put them back at the nurse's desk with specific instructions for each patient, Jacob approached her. As she turned to leave, she nearly bumped into him. "Sorry, Jacob. Didn't realize you were there," she apologized and made to go around him as she was anxious to get out to Warrenton for Raphael's game. He blocked her way and instead took her arm and led her to his office on the pretense of needing to consult about a patient. Reluctantly, Jennifer followed.

As they sat down in his office, he coolly commented on her changed behavior. Jennifer could tell he was not happy about something but was not in the mood to wait around to find out why. He continued, "Normally, I would be ecstatic seeing you so smiling and downright jovial with the staff and patients." His tone indicated he was not ecstatic at all. Quite the opposite. "However, it seems after you lost your patient just yesterday that perhaps you would become less distracted and refocus on saving the others instead of happily humming as you complete paperwork." His objective was clear – make her doubt herself and refocus the blame on the patient's death on her to guilt her into leaving behind whoever was diverting her attention from her work even for a second.

At first she was bewildered that he considered her to be unfocused on her patients and her work. After a few moments thought, she realized he could be right. Even she was astutely aware that ever since she had reconnected with Lorenzo, she found her mind drifting to him. Jennifer had convinced herself it was only when she was away from the hospital and not that often. After last night's events, maybe it had been more than that and she just hadn't realized it. Observing the look of doubt cross her face, Jacob went in for the kill. "Perhaps you need something to fire your motivation for your research. There's a fundraiser tonight at Smithsonian. Why don't you come with me? You can redouble your efforts if more money is flowing in for research." Sadly defeated, she shook her yes and left the office. Jacob sat back in his chair with a smug smile.

Her new found pep vanished as she exited the hospital. "He was right," she chided herself, "I could've saved that suffering child if I had just spent more time at the hospital, more time researching the new protocol so it could've been used before it was too late. This was all my fault. What was I thinking that I could have a personal life now? I've done without one for years. Obviously I don't need a man or love, and certainly not a family. My life's work is at a crucial stage. I can't allow myself to be diverted any longer. I owe it to the other children in that ward. Despite her heart and body screaming their need for Lorenzo, she resolved to end things with him before she lost the will to do so.

Tears rolled down her freckled face as she dialed Lorenzo's number. It went straight to voicemail so she left a short message saying there had been some complications at work and she would be unable to make Raphael's game. Unable to hold herself together when he called back just a few moments later, she turned off her phone and headed back home. The condo seemed so much lonelier without him. She thought, "Has it really only been a few hours since Lorenzo was here holding her, kissing her, making love to her?" It seemed like a lifetime ago now.

Without feeling much like going to a party, much less a charity event with Jacob, she dressed in a subdued gray chiffon number that fell off one shoulder. She may look dazzling but she didn't feel the part. Jennifer just went through the motions that evening. Smiling when talking with potential donors. Allowing Jacob to usher her around the room as his own personal property. She was even caught unawares when he introduced her to a high-ranking senator as his girlfriend. It jolted her out of her reverie like being struck by lightning. Unwilling to make a scene or embarrass him in front of the party guests, she continued to smile even when the senator made a remark to Jacob about not letting such a beauty get away. Jacob, of course, was in agreement with the suggestion.

Later that night, his car dropped Jennifer off at her condominium building. Jacob tried to convince her to invite him upstairs for nightcap and perhaps more. The entire ride back he had spent making allusions to how they made such a great "power couple". Not in the mood to deal with him and not wanting to risk her job at the hospital by giving him a piece of her mind, she bolted from the car without as much as a goodbye. "How could she have allowed him to manipulate her like that?" she wondered. It took his antics tonight to reveal the creep underneath. He wasn't worried about her neglecting her patients or research. He was only concerned about alienating her from everyone else so she would be vulnerable to him. How could she not have seen it before? Racking her brain for signs that she had missed, she recalled overhearing some nurses commenting about "poor sweet doctor" being preyed upon by "the big guy" and being completely oblivious. They had been talking about her, hadn't they? Honestly, Jennifer didn't know who she was more angry with...Jacob for pushing doubt into her mind that she was not a good doctor because she wasn't focused enough on her work and making her believe it was her fault patients died or herself for believing him. She had denied herself any life for years due to her own self-doubts. He had merely amplified that doubt and handicapped her emotionally so she wouldn't stray from her work, stray from his sight and control. Perhaps the best place to lay her anger was at her own feet for allowing it to happen.

She was so caught up in her inner rage that she didn't see the tall shadow come up behind her as she opened the front door to the building. It wasn't until she moved into the building and saw a muscular arm reach out to hold the door open that she turned around in fright. She was shocked to see Lorenzo standing in the doorway with an anguished look. What he was thinking she couldn't guess. They had made plans to be together that day and she had wimped out by leaving him a message with no explanation. Now here she was dolled up from her night on the town with her boss. They stood in the vacant foyer staring at each other in the dark for several moments before Lorenzo turned to leave without saying a word. Desperate to explain, she reached for him but he flung her arm back.

As he brusquely walked out the door, a pouring rain had just started. Jennifer rushed out to stop him, but he continued briskly walking to wherever he had parked his SUV. Unable to keep up in her 2 inch heels, she stopped only long enough to pull them from her feet. The shoes were left there as she raced after him. Even though she was a fast runner and had placed in the last Marine Corps marathon, Jennifer found it difficult to keep up. As he neared his car, she dashed across the street unaware of an approaching taxi. The last thing she saw was Lorenzo's look of horror as he turned to see the collision. Then everything went dark.

Jennifer awoke to a throbbing in her head and the incessant beeping of heart rate monitor. Placing her hand to her head and feeling the large lump, she moaned in pain. The sound awakened the sleeping giant beside her bed. Despite everything, Lorenzo had stayed with her. Her mind was still too fuzzy from the accident that she couldn't begin to understand why after she had ditched him and his son last night. Perhaps he could forgive her not showing up for him, but letting Raphael down – she doubted anyone could forgive that. She certainly didn't forgive herself.

Lorenzo took her hand and asked how she felt. Instead of saying the expected response like "fine" or "horrible" or any derivative of the two, she simply said "stupid". Thinking she meant stupid for running out into the street in front an oncoming car, he nodded agreement. "Haven't you heard of looking both ways before you cross the road?" he challenged.

Her head still groggy and her thoughts jumbled, she tried to explain that it wasn't being hit by the car that was stupid. It was how she had convinced herself that she was a horrible person for wanting a life, wanting him and his son in her life instead of spending every waking moment under Jacob's thumb at the hospital. She tried explaining how he had manipulated her into doubting her dedication to her patients and guilted her into going to a hospital fundraiser instead of where she belonged at Raphael's game. It was stupid to believe she couldn't be a good doctor if she allowed herself to have anything or anyone else in her life. It was stupid not to realize that she wanted, that she needed love too. And it was stupid of her not to realize all this time that she needed and loved him.

By the time she finished speaking, they were both in tears. The nurse came in to check on her patient to find the doctor and her hot looking companion holding each other as if for dear life. She recognized the signs, so she quickly and quietly left in order to disturb the lovebirds.

As she was signing her release papers, Jacob stopped by her room. Lorenzo recognized him as the gentleman that had dropped Jennifer off the night before. He certainly didn't like the way the man was looking at her. By the expression on her face, Jennifer wasn't happy to see him but she motioned for Lorenzo to wait outside.

Jacob tried apologizing for not walking her in, as if that would have prevented the accident. Unable to contain her emotions any longer she let into him for all the years he had spent parading her around like an ornament at charity events. All the while belittling her work and making her doubt her own dedication and ability to saving children's lives. It had all been for his benefit. With her by his side he could raise money supposedly for her research, but she never saw a dime of that money. She was always scrapping by with used equipment and no personnel. Despite the odds, she still made significant progress. Exhausted from her long overdue rant against him, she verbally gave him her notice of resignation. She would take her research and skills to another hospital.

After he left, Lorenzo returned awestruck by what he had heard through the thin glass doors. Apparently, the entire floor had heard her accusations as there was applause from the nurse's station as Jacob stormed off to his office. With a look of admiration, he shook his head. "Well, does this mean you have some time to hang out with a young man who is desperately waiting to hear the news that you are okay, and with his old man?"

"After all this, do you really still want me around? It's not like we can just go back to the other night and pretend none of this happened," she replied.

"Yes, WE," he emphasized, "want you around. And not just for a soccer game. Not just as an overnight guest. Not as just a convenient date for weddings." Holding her bruised face in his hands, he looked into her eyes and confessed, "I want you, need you in my life. Ever since college, I've been in mad love with you but knew you didn't feel the same. For years I hid behind the status of friend. Too afraid to speak up even when you took off for medical school." He continued as she stared at him in disbelief, "Seeing you again brought all those feelings rushing back but you still showed no signs of wanting anything other than a platonic friendship. You were only focused on your work. I understand your need to help save lives. I understand your desire to find the cure so other children don't have to suffer like your friend Hannah. I understand all that and love you for all that and more. You've just been too blind to see it," he confessed.

Whoa! Jennifer didn't trust her ears on that last part. "Did he just say 'love'?" she questioned herself. With new tears rolling down her face, she nearly punched him. "Love? You've been in love with me and never said a word? Are you sure you don't want to take that back? Better do it quickly before I hold you to that." In reply, he pulled her close. The kiss that followed was soft, yet deep and all-consuming.

The pounding in her head was no more. The only pounding she felt was her own heart. She pulled back for just a moment to ask, "And how does Raphael feel about all this?"

A few months later in Dallas, Lorenzo and Raphael escorted Jennifer into the wedding ceremony for Kyle and his bride. Ever since that day in the hospital they had been together. She had been true to her word and resigned from Georgetown University Hospital. After taking some much needed and deserved time off, she had just accepted a job offer at a private research facility and hospital being built on the outskirts of the DC metropolitan area as their director of pediatric cancer research. The condo in Georgetown sold quickly, as the district never suffered from the housing market bust like the rest of the country. Presently, she was renting a townhouse in Warrenton so she could be close to "her boys".

Her relationship with Raphael had bloomed quickly. They were completely attached to each other. Even the blonde teacher's assistant that had been so rude to her at the other wedding admitted that Jennifer was devoted and loving to the boy. The soccer team adopted her as the team "mom" as she always brought them healthy snacks and tended to their bumps and bruises. There had been one instance where Raphael had been hit in the head with the ball so hard that he was knocked out for a few moments. Jennifer hadn't realized until then just how much she had grown to love him as she begged and pleaded with God for Raphael to wake up and be okay. He was, of course, but she could no longer deny she wanted to be a mother to him.

As for her relationship with Lorenzo...Jennifer wanted to kick herself every day for being blind to his feeling for her for so long, and blind to her feelings for him. He didn't allow her to wallow in regret though. The time was much better spent making up for lost time, which happen to include making lots and lots of love. Despite their need to be together, she insisted on keeping her own apartment. She didn't want Raphael to be upset having another woman sleeping his dad's bed. If they have bothered to ask, Raphael would have gladly told them otherwise.

Jennifer could not believe how blessed she was having Lorenzo and Raphael in her life. As she sat in the church pew flanked on both sides by the men she loved and listening to the words being said by the priest about love and family, she finally realized just how important those things were. Nearly missing her opportunity for true love gave her a greater appreciation for the words being spoken for the bride and groom. Lorenzo wasn't just her wedding date. He wasn't just her boyfriend. He and his sweet son were her life.

After the lovely ceremony, the wedding party adjourned to the large, heated tent erected on the local minor league baseball field. Turns out Kyle's company did considerable business with the team's owner who had loaned them the location for the reception. After dinner and dancing, Raphael was showing signed of fatigue so they decided to return to their hotel. Lorenzo seemed reluctant to leave and then excused himself for a moment. Confused, she stayed with Raphael as they waited for their coats.

A few moments later the strands of Frank Sinatra's "The Way You Look Tonight" began to play. Lorenzo returned and without a word ushered Jennifer out onto the dance floor for one final dance. Raphael stood just to the side of the dance floor watching them intently. As she leaned her head against his chest and listened to his heart thumping she became concerned it was beating so quickly. Towards the end of the song, Lorenzo dropped to one knee and gazed up at her with such a mixed expression of fear and longing. She didn't immediately notice the small box he had pulled out of his suit jacket. Confused, she stared in disbelief as the music faded away and Lorenzo uttered the words he had been waiting years to say to her. "Jennifer, my love, you are my heart and soul. I can no longer live without you. I want, I need you as my wife and my partner in life. Raphael wants and needs you as his mother." With that the boy ran over to the couple looking up at her with the most beautiful expectant expression. Lorenzo continued, "Jennifer, will you marry me?"

There it was. The question she hadn't realized she had wanted to hear so badly. Almost unable to speak, she looked into Raphael's face and then Lorenzo's and she knew that she was home. With happy tears streaming down her face, "Yes," she whispered, "yes."

******

Take Me Back

Although Mike had broken up with her 3 years earlier, Gia Russo hoped for a reconciliation. Mike had long since moved on with another women, while Gia, a cosmetologist, avoiding dating. When they first broke up, Mike questioned his decision to end the relationship, but in the end, he felt that he made the right decision.

The couple met when Mike came into the hair salon where Gia worked, to get his hair cut. She thought he was the sexiest guy she ever met, but felt that he was "out of her league." Mike was a partner in a large law firm who played polo, was a member of a posh country club, and who traveled all over the world.

Gia came from a blue-collar family, whose father was a truck driver. Her mother was a stay-at-home mom, but worked part-time, "doing hair" in the basement of their modest home.

While in high school, Gia excelled in math and science, but her family was unable to afford her college tuition. She wanted to become a nurse, or even a doctor, but her dreams were dashed when her father got laid off from his job.

Gia had to go to work to help support the family, and in her spare time, she decided to go to beauty school. She paid for her beauty school tuition out of the money she made from working at the local hardware store, and after about a year, she passed the state boards to become a licensed cosmetologist.

On Gia's 25th birthday, her friends took her out to a local bar to celebrate. Although she met a few eligible guys that sparked her interest, she couldn't get Mike out of her mind. All she could do was hope that he would make a second appointment for a hair cut, and return to the salon.

As luck would have it, Mike returned to the salon a couple months later, and to Gia's complete surprise, he asked her out. Their first date took them to Mike's country club, where Gia met his friends.

Mike was 10 years older than Gia, although he acted much younger. Even though Mike acted young and vibrant, she found his friends to be boring, stodgy, and arrogant. Despite her disdain for his friends, she quickly fell in love with Mike. He treated her like a queen, and even offered to pay for her to go back to college.

The couple soon settled into a mundane dating routine, and although Gia was still happy, she could sense that Mike was becoming restless. He seemed irritated and distant with her, and started going out a few times a week.

Most of Mike's family members liked Gia, however, his mother never warmed up to her. She never thought that Gia was good enough for her son, but remained cordial to her.

Mike's mother, Dina, on more than one occasion, tried introducing her son to various women. These women were all professionals, and a few were attorneys, just like her son.

Mike's father, Jack, also an attorney, stayed out of his wife's matchmaking schemes, as he was in his own little world, with a mistress of his own and a huge drinking problem.

Mike didn't invite Gia to his grandmother's birthday party, and when he arrived, he was greeted at the door by one of the most beautiful women he'd ever seen. He never saw her before, and wondered who she was there with. Little did he know, his mother invited her in an attempt to get him interested in someone other than Gia.

Her plan worked. Mike and the other women, whose name was Melissa, hit it off almost instantly. He couldn't stop looking at her, and was intrigued by her New York accent.

Melissa worked as an entertainment attorney, who represented a number of big name sports and music personalities. She even invited Mike to a sporting event which had been sold out for weeks.

Even though Mike had no intentions of breaking up with Gia, he could no longer ignore his feelings for Melissa. They soon started having lunch dates at 5 star hotels, and even managed to plan a getaway weekend to the Poconos.

When Mike started becoming increasingly distant from Gia, she started to suspect the worst. By this time, Melissa was pressuring Mike for a commitment. Although they've only been seeing each other for about a month, their relationship was growing more and more intense.

The sex was amazing, and Mike never experienced anything like it before. Melissa was willing to try new things in bed, and seemed to want sex multiple times a day. Gia, by contrast, was rather modest, and her sexual appetite was diminished by her escalating depression, and the side effects from the medication she was taking.

As the months passed, Gia was getting ready to go to Florida for a hair show. She and Mike were drifting further and further apart, but they still managed to maintain a dim spark of excitement between them. On the evening before she was schedule to leave for her trip, Gia and Mike went out for a romantic dinner, and then came home and spent the next three hours making love.

After their love fest, Mike turned over and went to sleep. Gia, the eternal romantic, want to cuddle, but Mike rebuffed her advances. The next morning, Mike drove Gia to the airport, and he couldn't help but feel profound relief. He would now be able to spend the next week with his new "friend," Melissa, and called her as soon as Gia boarded the plane.

For almost the entire week that Gia was on her business trip, Mike stayed with Melissa at her downtown apartment. The couple enjoyed cooking dinner together and waking up next to each other. Mike didn't know how he would tell Gia that he no longer loved her, and he even wished that she would stay in Florida for the long-term.

He was not responsive to her text messages, and only took her phone calls sporadically during that entire week. The week flew by quickly, and before he knew it, Mike found himself at the airport once again, but only this time, he was picking Gia up. She was elated to see him, but he cringed when they hugged.

Gia sensed that something was wrong, and was starting to worry. Mike told her that he was tired because he spent the entire week working on a brief for an upcoming legal case.

The couple trudged through the holidays together, but as Valentine's Day approached, Mike could no longer suppress he desire to be with Melissa. Although he knew that Valentine's week was not the most appropriate time to break up with Gia, he felt it was necessary, because he wanted to spend Valentine's Day with Melissa.

He didn't bother with formalities, and simply blurted it out. He told Gia that he was no longer happy with her, but didn't volunteer any information about his other woman. He further explained that he just needed time to be "by himself," and that "maybe" he would come to his senses and come back home to be with her. After Gia pressed him for answers, he finally came clean about Melissa.

After hearing the news, Gia broke down, and didn't think she would be able to function at work the next day. Of course, Mike told her that he didn't mean for it to happen, but when he met Melissa, an instant connection was made.

He didn't really want to divulge so much information about how he felt about Melissa, but he felt that unless he "drove his point home," Gia wouldn't take him seriously.

Gia was blindsided by the breakup. She tried to keep busy with work and going out with friends, but she couldn't shake the despair she felt. Although she was asked out on dates, she always declined.

In Gia's eyes, nobody would ever hold a candle to Mike, and she had no desire to date anyone because she knew it would never progress into anything further. In the meantime, Mike and Melissa were seen around town at various restaurants and social events.

On one occasion, Gia caught a glimpse of the couple getting out of a cab. This almost pushed her over the edge, but she managed to hold onto her dignity. After three years passed, Gia's feelings for Mike were still as intense as they were when they first started dated.

Mike's feelings for Gia, on the other hand, were almost non-existent. Sure he had fond memories of their time together, but never really felt as though Gia was his soul mate.

Gia eventually started seeing a counselor because she was not bouncing back from the breakup. Her sleep pattern was disrupted, her diet was poor, and she stopped socializing altogether. The only social stimulation she got was when she went to work, and even there, her social interactions were severely limited.

The counselor was worried for his patient's safety, and feared that she was spiraling into a deep, dark depression. Gia was eventually referred to a psychiatrist, who adjusted her medication and sent her on her way. When the medication kicked in after a few weeks, Gia's mood brightened, and she started considering dating again.

Gia met a nice guy at the gym, and when he asked her out for coffee, she felt flattered. Like Mike, Jason was older, distinguished and well-educated. Their coffee date was pleasant, but according to Gia, there was no spark.

When Jason asked her out for dinner, Gia hesitated, but decided to give him another chance. She was very critical of other men, but hoped that she would once again, find love. Jason took Gia to dinner and a play, and as the date was coming to a close, Jason leaned in for a kiss.

Gia had no intentions of kissing him, and in fact, she had no intentions of ever seeing him again. All she could think about was Mike. Three years have passed, and still, her love was as strong as ever.

Gia's co-workers were worried about her, and when she had too much to drink one night and drunk dialed Mike, they really became concerned. Fortunately she hung up before he answered the phone, but her number showed up on his caller ID.

Mike was curious to find out what Gia wanted. His relationship with Melissa was starting to cool, and lately, he started thinking about how much Gia loved him when they were together. He hesitated at first, but after a couple days, Mike returned Gia's call.

You could have knocked her over with a feather when she saw Mike's number come up on her caller ID. She was shaking as she answered the phone, and as soon as she heard his voice, she broke down sobbing.

Something stirred in Mike's heart, because he too, felt tears welling up in his eyes. Their phone call was brief, and in fact, it lasted only seconds, because Melissa walked into the room just as Gia answered. Mike took this as a sign.

Gia knew that Mike still felt a connection to her. She quickly put that phone call out of her mind, and tried to focus on her job. She went on a few more dates, and much to her surprise, Gia found a guy with whom she clicked with.

Her friend introduced her to an accountant who was from the same town that Gia was from. In fact, they lived within a few blocks of each other when they were teenagers, but they went to different schools. He went to a private, all-boys school, and Gia went to a public school.

At first, the relationship progressed slowly, but after a few months, Gia started developing strong feelings for her new friend, whose name was Mauricio. He took Gia to meet his family in Florida, and they absolutely loved her. Unlike Mike's mother, Dina, Mauricio's mother, Patty, felt that they were the perfect couple.

As their relationship grew stronger, Gia's feelings for Mike were becoming distant memories. In fact, days went by where she didn't even think about Mike at all. Mike, on the other hand, couldn't get Gia out of his mind. His relationship with Melissa was hanging by a thread, and he yearned for the relationship he once shared with Gia.

He was starting to realize that breaking up with her was a mistake, and he hoped that she was not involved with another man. Mike finally raised enough courage to call Gia back, and when she answered, his heart stopped.

He almost hung up, but was able to whisper out a weak, "Hi Gia, how are you?" Gia was gracious and warm, and replied, "Hi, Mike, it's nice to hear from you."

The conversation was strained and awkward, but in Mike's mind, the ice had been broken. He was certain that he could get back into Gia's good graces once again, so that they could pick up where they left off. Their conversation consisted solely of small talk, and neither one asked about the other's personal life.

Gia almost felt sick to her stomach when she heard Mike's voice, because it brought back the painful memories of their breakup. She was grateful that she had Mauricio, because he filled the void that Mike left. When she told Mauricio that Mike called, he became suspicious.

Why, he thought, would Mike call Gia, out of the blue, after three years apart. Did Gia initiate the first call, he wondered? Gia finally confessed to Mauricio that she did, indeed, "drunk dial" Mike days before.

It seemed that now, the tables were turned. Mike was the one who was pining away for Gia, while Gia, on the other hand, was blissfully "in like" with someone else. It never occurred to Mike that Gia would move on and start a new life with someone else. He also felt that Gia was his "ace in the hole," in case his relationship with Melissa didn't work out. Would he and Gia ever reconcile, he wondered?

Even though Gia was happy with Mauricio, she couldn't get Mike out of her mind, and wanted to connect with him again, just to find out more about his relationship status with Melissa.

Gia felt a twinge of guilt for thinking about calling Mike because Mauricio had been so good to her. She didn't want to be shady or go behind his back, so she talked to him about her intentions.

Gia felt that she needed to get Mike out of her system once and for all before she would be able to move forward with her relationship with

Mauricio. A total commitment to Mauricio was out of the question, in Gia's mind, unless she was completely over Mike.

Mauricio agreed that Gia needed to get Mike out of her system before they could take the next step in their relationship, so he encouraged Gia to make the phone call. Feeling better now that she confessed her feelings to Mauricio about Mike, Gia picked up her phone and dialed Mike's number.

He answered on the first ring, and couldn't believe his good fortune that Gia was calling him. "I want to see you," Gia said, as soon as Mike answered the phone.

Mike was shocked, but elated. By this time, he and Melissa were barely speaking, and she was spending more and more time away from the apartment that they shared since the beginning of their relationship.

Gia and Mike planned to go out for dinner so that could talk. Both were excited, anxious, but uncertain about a future together. When Gia saw Mike for the first time in three years, she was surprised that her heart wasn't racing, and that she did not have butterflies in her stomach.

Although it was nice to see Mike, that intense spark of passion and love was not there. Mike, on the other hand, could barely contain his emotions, and started to cry when they hugged.

He apologized to Gia for hurting her, but she was unfazed. The cold and uncaring manner in which he "dumped" Gia always bothered Mike, but he never had the opportunity to tell Gia how he felt. They talked about Mike's relationship with Melissa, and how it started out so intensely, but then, over time, seemed to have burned itself out.

Gia listened quietly as Mike spoke about how Melissa was a workaholic, and how she never cooked a meal for him in three years. Not only didn't she cook, she never cleaned either.

Mike finally hired a cleaning service to come in twice a month to tidy up, but he wished that Melissa was a little more domesticated.

She wasn't into the "housewife" thing, and she certainly didn't have any maternal instincts either.

Gia couldn't help but feel a twinge of satisfaction while Mike was droning on about his faltering relationship with Melissa. Mike was the type of guy who enjoyed home-cooked meals, who liked a clean home, and who wanted to start a family some day.

Gia wanted to start a family too, but it was becoming more apparent to Gia, that instead of wanting to start a family with Mike, she wanted to start one with Mauricio.

Throughout the entire dinner, Mike talked about himself and his relationship with Melissa. He didn't ask Gia what was going on in her life until it was almost time for them to leave.

Mike was certain that Gia had been waiting around for him to come back all this time, and was profoundly disappointed when Gia told him that she had met someone else. What made Mike feel even worse was when Gia told him that she was falling in love with Mauricio.

Mike asked, "how could you have fallen out of love with me?" Gia replied, " It took a long time, but I finally found someone who appreciates me, embraces me for who I am, and whose family loves me." On one hand, Mike was happy for Gia, but on the other hand, he was jealous, hurt and angry.

How could he have let Gia go? He knew what a great woman she was, but he let his mother's silly opinion of Gia get in the way. Mike now realizes that Gia was the "one that got away," and his hopes of finding his one true love have been dashed.

As their dinner date was ending, Mike felt that he had lost Gia forever. He decided to swallow his pride and beg Gia for another chance. He realized the error of his ways, and vowed that if she would give him another chance, he would do everything in his power to make her the happiest women alive.

Although tempting, Gia gently declined. Her feelings for Mike had changed, and she knew that she would never be able to love him like she once had. Mike wouldn't let up on his request for another chance, and Gia, who kept politely turning him down, was getting increasingly aggravated by his persistence. Gia once thought that the sun rose and set on Mike, but now, she was beginning to see his true colors emerge.

Mike had always been on the arrogant side, and was accustomed to getting his way all the time. He was spoiled as a child, and always seemed to have the upper hand when it came to relationships. If he didn't get what he wanted, he became pushy, overbearing and selfish.

Mike was sure that if he kissed Gia, that old spark would re-ignite in her soul. Not only did Gia turn away from Mike's attempt at a kiss, she was repelled by it. He no longer had the same effect on her, and in fact, she wished that she could have snapped her fingers to bring her back home to Mauricio. She felt safe with Mauricio because he was so genuine and kind. There was not an arrogant or selfish bone in his body.

Gia always lived on the edge with Mike, and always questioned his feelings for her. She knows that Mauricio is in love with her, and only her. He is not on the lookout for someone better, or for someone who is on the same level as he is educationally. Even though Gia doesn't have a college education, she is extremely bright, quick witted, wise and perceptive. Qualities that Mike never saw in her.

He criticized Gia because of the way she spoke and because she never attended college. He wanted to pay for her college education so that she could "better herself," however, Gia believes that he only wanted her to go to college because he was concerned that she wasn't "scholarly" enough, and that it didn't look good for him to be with an "uneducated" woman.

Just to make sure that Mike was completely out of her system, Gia relented an kissed him. The kiss soon became more intense, and Gia could sense that Mike was getting overly enthusiastic.

Since she wasn't feeling the same way, she retreated. She now knew, for sure, that Mike wasn't the man for her. When she kissed Mauricio, passion stirs inside her, but when she kissed Mike, she felt nothing.

Although Gia felt guilty about kissing Mike, because she knew it would hurt Mauricio, she just had to know for sure if the excitement, love and passion were still there.

They were for Mike, but not for Gia. It was then and there, that she decided to say good-bye, once and for all. Gia would never turn back, and would finally close that chapter in her life.

After a year had gone by, Gia and Mauricio started planning their wedding. They were now totally committed to each other, and were living together.

Gia quit her job as a hair stylist, and was now working for Mauricio. This allowed them to spend all day together, which they cherished. Some couples enjoy the time they spend away from each other while they are both at their respective jobs, but for Gia and Mauricio, working together in the same office works well for them.

In addition to being soul mates, they are best friends, and can let their respective guards down when they are together.

Although Mauricio is technically Gia's boss, he never plays that card. He is also careful, however, to never show favoritism to Gia in front of his other employees.

He treats everyone with respect, and no one is treated better than anyone else. Many of Mauricio's employees have been with his for years, which is a true testament to his character. Gia is proud to be his life partner, both personally and professionally.

Gia was getting excited for her wedding, and before the big day, members of her bridal party gave her a bachelorette party. Gia almost forgot what it was like to have a good time with her friends, because the last time they all went out together, Gia was in a funk over Mike. She is grateful that her friends saw her through her ordeal, and is honored to have them be a part of her wedding day.

The celebration started off at a neighborhood bar where the ladies indulged in a few tropical drinks, then it was off to Gia's favorite restaurant. The night was exciting and fun, and Gia couldn't remember when she had such a fun time with her friends. The merriment came to a screeching halt in the blink of an eye, however. While the ladies were enjoying their dinner and each other's company, a familiar figure walked through the door.

It was none other than Mike. He was accompanied by an older woman, who Gia later recognized as his mother, Dina. The two looked solemn as they were seated at their table, and barely spoke to one another while they dined.

Mike and his mother hadn't yet noticed that Gia was at the restaurant, and Gia wanted it to stay that way. She didn't want anything casting a pall over her special evening, but when she had to go to the bathroom, she wondered how she'd sneak past their table without her cover being blown.

After thinking about it, she realized that she didn't care if they saw her or not. She didn't owe either one of them anything and didn't even feel obligated to greet them. Gia and her entourage made a beeline for the bathroom, but not before Mike's mother noticed them. "Isn't that Gia?" she asked.

Mike was stunned and took this as another opportunity to try and win her back. It's fate, he thought. Yes, it was fate, but not in the way that Mike had hoped for. He stalked the bathroom door and waiting for Gia to come out. When she did, he greeted her with a hug. Gia tried to be personable, but again, she couldn't hide her disdain for Mike.

Gia and Mike ended up having a brief conversation. Gia was more than happy to tell Mike about her impending nuptials to Mauricio. She then learned why Mike and his mother looked so stone-faced when they walked into the restaurant.

It turned out that Mike was the one who was now battling severe depression ever since Gia didn't return his affections the last time they had dinner together. In fact, his depression got so bad that he had to give up his law practice and move in with his mother.

This was the first night he had been out in public in months. His relationship with Melissa had long since fell apart, and he was having a hard time re-building his life. Gia felt bad for Mike, and now wondered if his mother felt any remorse for sticking her nose in their business by setting him up with Melissa.

Gia and Mauricio were married in a beautiful ceremony, and now have an adorable baby girl. Mike is still living with his mother, and has let his law license expire.

He did get a job working as a handyman in the neighborhood, however, and Gia has since shown pity on him and hired him to install a white picket fence around her and Mauricio's sprawling new home.

******

For Keeps

Scott Mitchell and Tiffany Reynolds have been best friends since grade school. Although Scott knew that he and Tiffany would never end up being a "couple," he always hoped that they would end up together one day. He was disheartened when Tiffany chose to move three thousand miles away to New York City to pursue a career in advertising. When Tiffany graduated two years earlier, Scott hoped she would have moved back home to the small California town in which they both grew up in.

However, that didn't happen, and because of this, Scott was only able to see Tiffany when she returned home during the holidays. This always put him in a sad mood because he wasn't able to see his best friend as much as he would have like to. While he had lots of guy friends, Scott never felt close enough to any of them to share his inner feelings in the same way he was able to do with Tiffany.

As the years dragged on, Scott slowly began realizing that it wasn't their best friend status that left him wanting Tiffany closer, it was the fact that he had true feelings for her and he never felt at ease to tell her.

That was all going to change and soon. He flipped open his cellphone and replayed her message:

"Hey, Scott. It's your BFF. I just wanted to let you know that I am heading back in town and I have some news for you...actually two pieces of news for you. I'm sorry that I missed you, but I will call you as soon as the plane touches down. Love you Scott. Talk to you soon!"

He disconnected the call. He didn't know why he saved it, but he just felt compelled to. That call came in twelve hours, four minutes, and thirty-three seconds ago. He couldn't wait to have her call back. "I am such a loser," he moaned to himself. "Here I am pining away for a girl that I wanted nothing to do with when we were ten years old. If I would have known then, what I know now." He said, shaking his head. He grabbed a change of clothes and went into the bathroom. He started the shower and got undressed.

As the water washed over him, he could hear the sound of his cell phone. He quickly stepped out of the shower, not caring that the water was still running. He wrapped a towel around his body and headed back into his bedroom, reaching the phone before it hung up. "Hello?"

"Scott?"

His heart skipped a beat, hearing her voice. "Tiff? I wasn't expecting your call so soon."

"Did I wake you?" She asked.

"No," he replied, sinking down on the bed. "I was just taking a shower." He cursed himself for being so vocal, when he heard the hesitation. "It's good to hear your voice, Tiff."

She chuckled. He loved the sound of her laughing. "You hear my voice all the time. I call you more than I call my mother."

"You know what I mean. It's great to hear your voice, knowing that you're back in California." He replied, crossing his fingers. "You are in California, right?"

"Yes, I am. The plane touched down about ten minutes ago. I told you that I would call you right away."

Scott smiled to himself. It made him feel good that he was the first call she made. "Do you need a ride somewhere? I could come get you and be there in less than twenty minutes." He looked down at his wet body and shrugged. He would take the fastest shower anyone has ever taken if he had to.

"That's sweet, Scott, but I'm going to get a rental. Thanks for the offer though."

"Sure, no problem," he states, a little disappointed.

The awkward silence builds and he fights the urge to talk too much, but he can sense something is on her mind. "So, what's new?" He asks, hoping it didn't come across as a strange question.

"A lot," she confesses. "In fact, I was hoping that maybe we could talk this evening for supper. If you're not busy."

He thought about his busy work schedule, but he could move some things around. "Tonight would be perfect."

"Great! I will plan on meeting at our place about 6:30."

He smiled, knowing that she meant *Uncle Tony's Pizzeria*. "I will see you then." He replied, disconnecting. He went back to his shower, feeling excited about the evening. He was ready to tell her the truth and hope for the best, or at least hope that she wouldn't choose to discontinue their friendship.

*****

Tiffany wrung her hands together. She could feel her heart thumping in her chest and she didn't know why she was so nervous. She glanced around the restaurant and saw that he was still not there. He was her best friend and the fact that she felt like she was getting ready to see a stranger was weird. They didn't see each other often, but when they did it was like they had never been apart.

She looked up and saw him rushing into the restaurant. She took a deep breath and stood up. He hurried to her. "I am so sorry for being late." He kissed her cheek, "It was a busy day at work."

"No problem. I wasn't worried. I knew you would show." She smiled at him. He looked at her and grinned. For a moment she was reminded how she grew up having the biggest crush on him and he never seemed to notice. She cleared her throat, "I figured we didn't need to look in the menu."

He smiled, "You would be correct." He looked at her, "You're looking good, Tiff."

She blushed, "Thanks. You don't look half bad yourself." Their easy banter would pick up. It always did. The waitress walked over and they ordered their usual Pineapple and Pepperoni pizza, something only the two of them would enjoy. She then turned back to him. "So, how have you been? Any new girlfriends I should know about?" She took a drink of her soda and he laughed.

"Not quite. You know me...I'm involved with my job. Isn't that enough?"

She thought about that. It was true that he did seem to be a workaholic, but he always found time to make for her. "I have a feeling when you find that someone special then that will all change."

He smiled, "Think so, huh?"

She nodded, confidently. "I actually have some things that I want to discuss with you."

"Hm..." he replied. "I thought this impromptu supper was because you missed me."

She shrugged, "Well, that's true too."

"Okay, I feel a little bit better," he spoke with a laugh. "I actually have some things that I want to discuss with you too."

"You do?" She asked, surprised.

"I do, but I thought maybe we could wait a little bit before I delve into that. So, feel free to begin."

She waited for a moment, trying to figure out how she wanted to proceed. She had been rehearsing the way she was going to tell him for several weeks now, but it all seemed to go out of her mind. "It can wait. How's your family been?"

He raised his eyebrows. "That's changing the subject, but they have been doing really well. Sid just started at the University and Bryce is a senior this year."

"Wow. That's hard to believe. I remember when they were just— "

"Pests...bothering us relentlessly?"

She laughed, "I was going to say that I remember when they weren't even in school yet. I feel old."

"Tell me about it," he replied, chuckling.

The waitress came with their food and they fell into an easy silence as they started to eat. "I really am excited that you're here."

She smiled, "Me too." She took another bite and figured she would wait until they were done eating, before bringing up the reason she was in town. "Has work been going okay?" She asked, stopping to take a drink.

"Busy as ever, but loving every minute of it. I should ask you how your jobs going? After all, working at a big time ad agency must have some perks."

She nodded, but barely made eye contact. "It's been great, but I actually quit there two weeks ago."

His jaw dropped, "Must not be that great. Why did you do that?"

She shrugged, "Had my reasons."

He put down his slice of pizza. "We have known each other for almost twenty years and have been best friends for fourteen of those years. You aren't going to get away with that. What happened?"

She groaned, taking her last bite of pizza. "I'm moving back to California."

"What? Are you serious? When were you going to tell me that?"

"Tonight," she replied nonchalantly. "I was waiting for the perfect moment. Are you surprised?"

"Um...yeah, I'm surprised." A smile is on his face, but then he starts to frown. "May I ask why? I mean you seemed so happy when you made the decision to stay there. What changed?"

She knew that it was the moment she had been practicing for. "Well...my fiancé is getting transferred." That wasn't exactly how she envisioned telling him, but it got the point across.

He stared at her and then shook his head, "I'm sorry, I thought you just said that your fiancé is getting transferred."

"That's exactly what I said. Surprise...I'm getting married."

She couldn't read his mind to see how he felt about the news. She knew that he wasn't expecting it, when she had only been dating Erick for a month. She hadn't even told her family or Scott that she was seeing someone. "When did this happen?" He asked.

"He proposed a couple days ago, but he asked me to move to California with him two weeks ago."

"I'm sorry that I am finding this a little hard to believe. I mean, up until about five seconds ago I didn't even know you were dating anyone. Now, to hear that you are moving to California with your fiancé? It's a lot to take in."

"I know," she replied quietly. "I didn't plan it. One day I was meeting him, the next day he was telling me that he loved me, then he was saying that he was getting transferred to California, and asking me to go with him. It just all happened so quickly, but I do love him."

"You do?" He replied softly.

She didn't need time to consider it. She knew that in her heart she felt love for him. "He gets me in ways that not too many people do." She looked down at her empty plate, "Similar to ways that you get me."

He nodded, taking another bite of his pizza. "Wow...I am just in shock."

She knew he would be, because outside of the occasional dating she never really was too involved with boys. She never seemed to have time for them, when she was too preoccupied with other things going on in her life. "Are you happy for me?" She asked, carefully considering the question.

He slowly nodded, but then added a smile. "Of course I'm happy for you. It's just going to take some time to get used to." He hesitated, looking down at the table, "When am I going to meet him?"

"He'll be in town in a few days." She said. "I wanted to prepare my family...and you, before you met him." She replied, but part of her still wondered why she was worried about what they would thing...especially Scott. She couldn't explain it, but she was most worried how Scott would react to him.

*****

Scott had to process the news. The minute Tiffany told him she was getting married, he found himself sick. They went on with their meal, like nothing was happening inside of him, but he was finding it difficult to concentrate. He wanted to be happy for her, but the thought of losing her to another guy was too much to bear.

"I am so relieved that you took the news this way." She was saying.

"Oh...why's that?" He asked, taking a drink.

She shrugs, "I don't know. I guess you're opinion matters to me." It was a simple response, but he questioned if that was all. "It was actually more difficult telling you, than it will be to tell my parents."

Scott slowly nodded and then glanced down at her finger. He didn't even want to bother asking why she wasn't wearing the ring. He figured she did that so that she could tell people, without having them see the ring first. "Maybe it's because I was your first husband." He frowned, "Come to think of it...did we ever officially get divorced? You might want to check into that, before you say you'll marry this guy."

Her eyes got big, but then she smiled and started to laugh. "The playground marriage, who could forget that?" She shrugged, "I'm pretty sure the marriage was dissolved the day that you carried Sissy Baker's books to her class in ninth grade." She shook her head and acted like she was crying, "It broke my heart."

He smiled, "She was a tough girl. She threatened to beat me up if I didn't carry her books." He winked at her and she laughed. "I was only trying to save my life." He thought on what he wanted to say next and his mind drifted back to his dream that he woke up to. "I have actually been thinking about that marriage." He admitted.

She smirked, "You have?"

He nodded, "Yep and it occurred to me that I don't even remember how it came about." He shrugged, "I guess it really doesn't matter, but it's something that I have wondered."

"You mean...you don't remember the undying love you had for me?" She took a piece of her pizza and shook her head, "I am hurt." She took a bite and he could see her smiling.

"I have to admit, I did have a thing for girls in pigtails." He replied, laughing.

She snickered and nodded, "I figured." She looked down at her plate and he could see that she was thinking about that day. "Don't you remember? You wanted to play on the monkey bars and I told you that I would only let you do that if we got married." She smiled, "I was pretty tough back then."

He thought about that and then the realization snuck in. He laughed, "That's right. The monkey bars get me all the time." He turned quiet and then looked at her, "You know, that was really the start of our friendship."

She raised her eyebrows and then nodded. "We've been close ever since."

He could see that there was something on her mind and he decided to try to find out what was going on. "I can tell something's bothering you."

"This won't change anything, Scott. We'll still be friends."

The way she said that, caused a knot in his chest. "I know we will. Just not best friends, because that will be reserved for your husband. I get that." He told her everything that he needed to tell her, but in his mind he was fumbling with the words. He was going to have a hard time getting over this.

*****

Tiffany laid in bed, her eyes were focused on a picture of Scott and her that they had taken in a mall photo booth. She wanted to believe that everything was going to be alright when it came to their friendship, but her head was telling her that nothing was going to ever be the same. Things at her parent's house went fine. They were happy for them and no doubts were left behind.

She heard her cellphone ringing and she reached it from the bed. She glanced at the caller ID and saw that it was Erick. She answered the call. "Hello?"

"Hey, babe." He said. "How was your first day back?"

She looked at the picture and then placed it on the hotel nightstand. "It went well." She smiled to herself, "When does your plane arrive?"

"Well, that's one of the reasons I was calling." He said. His voice sounded apologetic.

"Yes?" She asked.

"I just found out that the transfer isn't going to be finalized for two more weeks."

The phone nearly fell from her hands. "Are you serious?"

"I'm sorry Babe, but I have to stay here until that becomes definite."

She couldn't believe this was happening. "I came here now, because I thought that you would be following shortly behind." She looked around her hotel room, "What should I do here while I wait for you to arrive?"

"Well...maybe you could start looking for a house for us to live in. Plus, you still have to find a job."

She nodded slowly, "Fine," she said, knowing that the disappointment was there.

"Babe, don't be like that." He says. His voice held concern, but she wasn't at the point of worrying about that. "We will be together soon and it will be like we were never apart."

"I know," she sadly replied. "I will see what I can do without you here."

"I love you," he replied.

She let out a breath, "I love you, too. Goodbye." She hung up the phone and turned to the picture of Scott. She dialed up his number, hoping it wasn't too late. He answered quickly, showing that it wasn't a problem. "Hey, Scott."

"Hello...miss me already?"

She smiled to herself, "Not quite."

"Ouch, I'm hurt," he teased.

She rolled her eyes, "I was just calling to see what you were doing this weekend."

There was a hesitation on his end and she wondered if maybe she was too quick to jump to the conclusion that he wouldn't be busy. "Well, I..." he started, but she quickly broke in.

"I am sure you are busy. I didn't mean to be insensitive. You have a life. We can get together later."

"Tiffany, are you through?" He asked. She closed her mouth and didn't say anything else. "I have a lunch meeting with a client, but after that I have no plans. Did you want me to meet your fiancé? I hope," he replied, laughing.

"Well, not exactly. It turns out that he won't be coming back for a couple more weeks." She paused, "long story. I just thought that maybe we could go to some of the old places we used to go."

"Well, I think that that would be a fabulous idea." He replied. "I could pick you up at the hotel about two o'clock. If that works for you?"

"That would be great," she agreed. "See you in a few days. Goodnight."

"Goodnight," he said, as they disconnected the call. She put the phone back on the nightstand. She knew that beginning the following week she would need to start looking for that perfect job. She laid back in bed and closed her eyes. She would have plenty of things to do to keep herself busy, until Erick was arriving in California.

*****

Scott picked her up at two o'clock sharp. He didn't want to question why her fiancé wasn't going to be there until later. He didn't really care. He was happy to step in and show her a good time. He walked up to her hotel room door and knocked. She opened up the door instantly. Her smile always caught him off guard. She left the hotel room and glanced up at me. "Thank you for wanting to get together."

"Of course." They fell into an easy stride with one another.

"How did your meeting go today?" She asked.

He was always surprised with how much she seemed interested in what he was doing. "It went well. I signed him on with a contract." They left the hotel and walked to his car. He stood at the passenger side, opening the door for her.

"Thank you!" She replied, getting into his car. He hurried around to the other side. "Where are we going first?" She asked.

"I have my preferences, but I suppose it can be your choice." He said, hoping she would choose their favorite ice cream shop.

"You want dessert?" She asked.

He laughed, "You read my mind." He put the vehicle into motion and they headed toward their destination. "So, you were rather vague on the phone. Why isn't your fiancé coming to California yet?"

She looked out the window, like she didn't want to make eye contact. "His work put a delay on his transfer." She shrugged, turning to face him. "I guess that it gives me time to sort out of my life here. I have to find a job and I can start looking for houses."

"Alone?" He asked, trying not to butt in.

She nodded, "It might not be the best scenario, but I can always send him pics of what I find and get his opinion. Right?"

He could tell that she was trying to be stronger about it than she was letting on, but he couldn't make her feel worse. "Of course."

She smiled, turning back and glancing out the window. He felt for her and couldn't believe how her fiancé would be willing to wait this long to meet up with her. He had a hard time being that far away from her and they weren't even dating. He pulled into the ice cream shop and her demeanor instantly changed. She seemed happy. "This is exactly what I need. Marla's famous double scoop fudge—"

"Peanut butter ice cream sundae," he finished for her.

She nodded, "I can taste it already." They got out of the car and headed into the small building. The minute they were seated, the teenaged girl approached them.

"Hello, my name is Noelle. Would you like a menu?"

They both shook their heads, "That won't be necessary," Tiffany responded, ordering the two desserts. "Thank you!" She said, watching the girl walk away. "Remember when I worked here?" She asked, turning back to Scott. "The outfits haven't changed."

He laughed, "This place was hopping on Friday nights after football games, but you seemed to love it."

She nodded, "I did." As her words came out, he spotted Marla heading their way. Tiffany looked up and jumped to her feet. "Marla…" she pulled her into a hug. "I have missed you." When she parted, it looked like she had tears in her eyes.

"We have missed you too, When I saw the order, I just knew that it would be my two favorite customers." Marla spoke with a smile. She turned to Scott and nodded. "Scott, good to see you too."

"Thank you Marla…likewise."

"So, what brings you back to California?" Marla asked, focusing back on Tiffany.

"Well, I am moving back to town."

"Her fiancé will be joining her shortly," Scott said. When Tiffany looked at him, he wasn't sure if it was anger or shock that he said anything. He was leaning more toward anger.

"Fiancé?" Marla asked, looking down and noticing the ring on her left hand. Her jaw dropped. "Holy cow…what does he do for a living?"

"He's a lawyer and he is transferring the branch in town." She held out her hand and Scott caught himself looking at it again. Each time he thought about the fact that she was getting married, he cringed. He looked up, forcing himself not to look at her engagement ring. There was a smile on her face, but there was also sadness in her eyes. He could feel it.

"Well, congratulations." Marla turned back to me and smiled, "I must admit, I always thought maybe the two of you would end up together." She laughed, "Apparently, I am not destined to be a psychic." She grinned, "Glad to have you home."

She walked away and Tiffany took her seat. Her face was red and I watched her for a second, before clearing my throat and trying to lighten the mood. "It must be that darn wedding when we were ten. It has people all confused."

She looked up and laughed, "Is that it?"

He shrugged, "Makes perfect sense." He looked up and saw the ice cream heading to their table. "Perfect timing." The girl put the ice creams down. "Thank you," he said, handing Tiffany a spoon. "Dig in."

They each took a bite as Tiffany sighed. "Heavenly."

He took a bite and nodded in agreement. This was something that would take away all worries and doubts and nothing was going to change that.

*****

Tiffany waited by the car, as Scott disappeared. He gave no explanation, but said he had a surprise for her. They had just finished at the ice cream shop and it definitely took her mind off of the fact that Scott wasn't going to be there.

She saw Scott heading back to the car. He was on the phone as he approached her. "We'll be there. Thank you Veronica." He disconnected the call, "Get in."

"Who was on the phone?" She asked, inquisitively.

"We are going to pick you out the perfect home." He replied with a smile. "I'll explain on the way." Tiffany wasn't sure about that, but got in anyway. He began to explain immediately. "Veronica Baylor is one of my clients and one of the top notch realtors in the area. I called her and asked her to put together a list of houses and we're going to meet her at one of them."

Her jaw dropped, "We're what?"

He glanced at her, "You heard me."

"Yeah, I heard you, but I don't feel like this is such a great idea. I mean...this is something that I am supposed to be doing with my future husband." She shrugged, "Seems strange."

He shook his head, "It's not strange. He isn't here and I am. It's better than going out alone. Besides, maybe I can help you get the perfect price." He turned back to the road. She was still apprehensive, but decided to go with it. He continued driving, until he turned onto a secluded street. He pulled up in front of a house that had a sale sign in front of it.

She looked at the house and imagined living there. It was fairly good size, but she would have to check the inside out. She got out of the car and they headed up to the door. From the car in the driveway, she knew that the realtor was already there.

He opened the door and called out, "Veronica?"

A tall woman came out of a room, wearing a smile. "Hello," she held out her hand and Tiffany shook it.

"Hello," Tiffany spoke. She was looking around the entrance of the house.

"Thank you for meeting us on such short notice," Scott was saying.

"Not a problem. Let me give you both the guided tour."

They followed her, through another room where she introduced the living room. It was a nice size room and Tiffany could picture the type of furniture they would get and where it would go. "This is a nice room," Scott was saying and she nodded.

"I'll show you the kitchen." As she led the way, she looked back at them. "When are you both getting married?" She asked.

"Um..." she glanced at Scott, looking for some help to explain it to her, but he was just smiling. "We're not." She finally spoke. The realtor looked away and she playfully hit him. He laughed.

"Tiffany is getting married. We're just friends."

"Oh..." Veronica said, seeming unfazed. "This is a nice kitchen. Do you like to cook?"

She opened her mouth to speak, but Scott was speaking instead. "She makes great peanut butter and jelly sandwiches." He replied. She glared at him and she could see that he was having a wonderful time on her behalf.

Veronica glanced back at her and Tiffany snickered, "I do alright in the kitchen." She turned and snared in his direction. "You are dead," she whispered.

He raised his eyebrows, but brushed past her as they entered the kitchen. "The best part of the house is the majority of appliances are staying."

"Why is the seller selling?" She asked, glancing at the nicely decorated room.

"She is getting older and her daughter lives out of town, so she decided to move closer to her daughter. She doesn't want a lot of her stuff."

"This is a nice kitchen," Tiffany mumbled, looking at the appliances. They each seemed fairly new. The tiled floor was also something that she liked.

"We can go upstairs where you will see the two bedrooms and a bathroom." They followed her out of the kitchen. When they reached the staircase, she pointed to another door. "There is a half bath right there." She led the way up the stairs and they reached the floor. She opened the door and they entered the room. "This is the master bedroom. It has a bathroom attached." She looked all over the bedroom. It was bigger than her New York bedroom, at least by three times.

"This is nice," she replied, opening up closets and stepping inside. In the bathroom, she could see the sink was completely made of ceramic and also looked brand new.

"Wow..." Scott mumbled, stepping in behind her.

She looked at him and nodded, "Nice, huh?" She whispered.

He nodded, "Definitely nicer than my apartment."

She smiled, as they stepped out of the bathroom. They exited the bedroom and looked at the other two. They were about the same, just smaller. "This is nice. Really it is," she started. They headed down the stairs and Veronica turned to her when they reached the foyer. "I am almost too afraid to ask the asking price."

Veronica held up her finger and disappeared back into the kitchen. "This is nice, but it's going to be way too expensive," she whispered to Scott.

Veronica came back into the foyer and looked over the paper. "You are looking at $115,000."

Tiffany gasped, figuring that it would be something like that. She opened her mouth, but again Scott was interrupting. "I'm sure that is just the asking price."

Veronica nodded, "I am sure that the owner would negotiate."

Tiffany tried to smile, "I appreciate the offer, but in order for us to be able to afford it...we would have to agree to way less than that. I am sure that she won't agree to negotiate that much. Thank you, but we'll have to keep looking." She headed out of the house, not wanting to think about it for another minute.

Scott joined her and they got into the car. "Don't you want to at least try?"

She thought about that, but then shook her head. "We have only looked at one house. I am sure there will be much more to look at. Thank you!" He turned from her and they waited until Veronica's car pulled out of the driveway and they followed her. She had no doubt that there would be plenty of houses that they could look into.

*****

Scott dropped Tiffany back off at her hotel. He had one of the best times he could have even imagined just looking at houses with her. It felt like they were a couple that were getting ready to get married. He still didn't know how Erick could stand being away from her.

He got back home and threw his wallet and keys on the coffee table and crashed on the couch. He didn't know how he would pull it off, but he knew that he wouldn't feel right if he didn't try to win her heart. He couldn't give up without a fight.

He got off the couch and thought about ways to a woman's heart. He grabbed a notebook from the kitchen drawer and took a seat at the table. He began writing her a letter:

Dearest Tiffany:

I have tried numerous times to tell you what's in my heart, yet the words always fail me or you are with someone else. While this might not be the most opportune time, I feel that I have to be honest with you and myself. Since the first day I laid eyes on you, I knew that you were something special. It was after our fake marriage at the age of 10, that I began to realize that there was more to you.

You are beautiful inside and out and I have been blessed to call you my best friend, but over the years I have struggled with what's right and wrong. I have wanted to be happy for you and I am, to an extent. I have watched you pursue your dreams and I couldn't be more proud of that. I stood back and didn't say a word, when you chose to stay in New York City, even though my heart was being ripped from my chest. I hear news that you are getting married and I am left wondering how I could be so stupid.

I am asking you not to walk down that aisle, because what you need is and has always been right before your eyes. I love you, Tiffany and nothing is going to stop me from saying that. I have been too scared to admit it, but I am running out of time and this is my last hope. Please, give us a chance. You are everything I could ever want and I have to tell you that. I will remain by your side no matter what happens, but I am hoping that you can find it in your heart to say that you love me too.

Love,

Scott

He looks at the letter and almost crumples it up, but he can't. He spoke from the heart and that's all he could do. He did know that he couldn't give her the letter so soon. He would focus on other ways to get through to her and use the letter has a final piece. He closed the notebook up and left the kitchen. He needed to take a cold shower and try to put her out of his mind. It wouldn't be easy, but it was what needed to be done.

*****

Tiffany yawned as she filled out her third application online. She hoped that one of the employers called her. She was just about to hit submit, when she heard a knock on her hotel room door. She quickly hit submit and then went to the door. She peered outside to find a man holding a bouquet of flowers at her door. She opened the door and smiled. "Hello."

"Hello. Are you Tiffany Reynolds?"

"Yes," she replied, staring at the bouquet of pink roses. They were her favorite color of roses.

He handed the flowers to her. "Enjoy!" He smiled, turning and walking away from her.

She looked down at the flowers and carried them back into the room. She placed them on the table and leafed through the bouquet, until she found the car. She removed it and read what it said:

Tiffany –
You are more beautiful now than the first day I saw you.
I hope these brighten your day.

She flipped the card over. It wasn't signed. "They have to be from Erick," she assured herself. She smelled the bouquet and smiled. "They sure are gorgeous," she mumbled, placing them on the table to brighten up the room. She heard her cellphone ringing and looked down to see that Scott was calling her. "Hey, Scott."

"Hey...what are you doing?"

She looked back at her computer and groaned, then looked at the flowers. "Staring at the most beautiful bouquet of roses. Erick knew the pick me up I needed." There was silence on the other end that she thought she had gotten disconnected. "Are you there?"

"Uh yeah...I'm here."

"So...what's up?" She asked, getting back to the reason he called.

"I thought maybe we could go out for lunch. I have some extra time, before having a meeting this afternoon."

"Sure, that would be great."

"Okay, meet you at my work at noon?"

"I'll be there," she replied. "See ya then," she hung up the call and looked back at the roses. She dialed up Erick's number. It went straight to his voicemail. She waited for the beep and then spoke, "Hey, babe...I just wanted to call you and tell you how much I love you and I miss you. I'm sure you're busy getting things finished up for work, but I can't wait to talk to you. Goodbye." She hung up the call. She wanted to hear his voice and thank him for the beautiful flowers, but it could wait. She walked back to the computer and closed it up. She would give it some time before applying for any more positions. She needed to get ready for lunch.

*****

Scott couldn't concentrate. He should have known that she would assume the roses were from Erick. He groaned in frustration, tossing his pen. "What did this pen do to you?" He looked up to see Heather, his receptionist, standing in the door.

"Oh...thanks." He said, taking the pen from her. He hesitated, before looking up at her. "You're a woman."

"Thanks for the brilliant deduction," she replied with a laugh.

He smiled, "I just meant, out of curiosity what do women like to receive as gifts?"

"Flowers," she stated, with conviction.

"Been there...done that," he replied. "What else?"

She seemed to ponder on that. "Well, you can't go wrong with candy...chocolate especially." He had thought about that, but he was trying to get away from the usual gifts. He chose flowers, because he knew how much she loved pink roses. "Jewelry is always a plus." She replied, smiling. "I guess that most women really just go for something that comes from the heart." She shrugged, "Doesn't have to take a lot of thought, but it needs to be real."

He nodded, trying to think about that. Some ideas entered his mind and he thought that he would have to try them out. "Thank you. Now, did you need something?"

"I was going to let you know that I was going out for lunch. Do you need anything?"

"Nope, I will be heading out soon. Enjoy."

She smiled. She turned around, nearly running into Tiffany. "Hey, Heather." They hugged one another, but when they parted Heather turned back to me. A look of recognition in her eyes. I tried to ignore her, turning to Tiffany.

"Tiffany, I hear that congratulations is in order." She stuck her hand out, showing Heather. I had to roll my eyes, because I was getting tired of dwelling on it. "That is a beauty." She glanced back at Scott, "It's a beauty, isn't it Scott?"

Scott nodded, "It sure is." He stood up and walked to the door. "Are you ready to go?"

"I better get going," Heather said.

"Goodbye, Heather." He called, as she left the office. "Where do you want to go?"

She shook her head, "I don't care."

They headed to the door and left the building. As they walked down the street to the corner restaurant, she began talking about the flowers. He wanted to ask if she was trying to make him jealous, but decided against it. He opened the door for her and she entered. "How did he sign it?" He asked.

She turned to him, "That's kind of private, don't you think?"

"Oh excuse me," he replied, sarcastically. He walked up to the podium and the hostess had them follow her. When they sat down, he looked at the menu. "If you have some cute name for each other and you don't want to tell me how he signed it, then more power to you." He looked through the menu, hoping she would see that he wasn't bothered by her words; even though he was.

"It's not that. In fact he didn't even sign his name. It was the words that meant the most. That's all."

He looked up at her, "If he didn't sign his name, how do you know that he sent them?"

She laughed, "Who else would send them?"

He shrugged, "I don't know. I was just curious." He looked back at the menu, knowing that he needed the conversation to be dropped. "I'm starving," he said, changing the subject.

She looked in the menu and he casually glanced at her from the corner of his eye. He hoped that the next attempt went more smoothly, because he was bombing out.

*****

Tiffany received a call, right after she got out of the shower. She didn't recognize the number, but since she had submitted so many applications she knew she needed to answer it. "Hello?"

"Hello, is this Tiffany Reynolds?"

"Yes, this is she." She said, crossing her fingers.

"Hello, Ms. Reynolds. This is Matthew Riley from Riley advertising. How are you doing?"

She could barely find the words. She couldn't believe the owner was actually calling her. "I...I'm doing great." She replied, trying not to sound too eager.

"Good to hear. I was hoping you could come in today so we could talk. I have received your application and I am very impressed." She could have squealed with pleasure, but she held back.

"That would be great. What time works best for you?"

"How about coming by at eleven o'clock. Do you know where we're located?"

She nodded, realizing that he wouldn't be able to see the gesture. "I do. I will be there. Thank you!"

"You're welcome. See you soon!" The call was disconnected and she stared at the phone. She twirled around her hotel room. She was hoping that this was the break she was looking for. She glanced at the clock, she had two hours to get ready and be there. She knew that it was about thirty minutes away, so she would have plenty of time. She grabbed her classiest outfit she had packed and got dressed. She spent more time on her hair and makeup. She wanted it to be perfect.

She was putting her earrings in, when she heard a knock . She rushed to the door and peeked outside. A guy was standing at her door. She frowned, but then flung the door open. "Hello?"

"Ms. Reynolds?" He asked. She nodded, "Please sign here." He handed her a clipboard. She signed her name and then he handed her a small box. "Have a nice day."

"You too," she replied, absentmindedly. She looked at the package and saw that there was no return address. Her name and the hotel address was handwritten on the front. She recognized the writing, but couldn't immediately place it. She opened up the box and found another box inside. This time it was a velvet box. She opened it up and stared at the necklace. Her eyes got big, finding the gold cross inside. Wrapped around the cross was rubies that alternated with topazes. She pulled it from the box. "It's gorgeous," she spoke, putting it around her neck and going to the mirror. "Perfect to complete the ensemble." She couldn't believe how thoughtful Erick was. His birthday was in

November, representing the topaz birthstone and her birthday was in April, representing the ruby. She ran her hand over the cross.

She had yet to hear back from him when she received the flowers a few days earlier. She picked up the phone and dialed his number again. Again it went straight to his voicemail. "Hey, Erick. I am starting to worry a bit. I haven't heard back from you in a few days. Thank you so much for the necklace. It's gorgeous. Also, the flowers were perfect. I love you." She hung up and glanced one more time in the mirror. She was ready to go land the job.

She called a cab and fifteen minutes she was out the door and heading to Riley Advertising. She was relieved to see that she wasn't nervous. She was anxious though. She paid the cab driver and hurried up the front steps. She was glad that she had brought her portfolio along. She felt professional and ready to make her move.

She approached the desk with confidence. "My name is Tiffany Reynolds. I am here to meet with Matthew Riley."

"Of course, Ms. Reynolds. He will be out in a few minutes. You may have a seat."

She sat down and waited for him to arrive. Like clockwork, it was only a couple of minutes. He walked out with swag, offering his hand to her. "Ms. Reynolds, it is very nice to meet you."

"Likewise," she spoke, standing up. She followed him, past the reception desk.

"Please hold my calls," he stated to the receptionist. They entered a room and he held back for her to go before him. "Please, have a seat."

She took a seat and placed her portfolio down. "I want to thank you for taking the time out to meet with me."

He smiled, "I have made some calls and you have come highly recommended." He stated. "Your previous employer was sorry to see you go."

She blushed, "I had to make a tough decision. I enjoyed working there."

"May I ask why you chose to leave?"

She thought about that, letting out a slow breath. "My fiancé is getting transferred here. So, I had no choice."

He nodded, "It's a good reason." He looked down at her application. "I am very impressed with your resume. I am assuming you have samples of your work."

"Of course," she said, reaching down and opening her briefcase. She took out her campaigns and handed them to him. It was the first step of letting herself out there and she hoped that he liked it.

*****

Scott looked up to find Tiffany entering his office. A smile was present on her lips. He stood up. "This is a pleasant surprise." His eyes instantly went to her necklace. He could definitely see that she wore it well.

"I got a job," she said, throwing her arms around him.

He held her close, feeling how much he wanted that to be an everyday occurrence. "That is wonderful news, Tiff." She pulled away and there was so much happiness in her eyes. "I bet Erick is ecstatic."

Her eyes fell to the ground, "He probably would be if I could get ahold of him." She shrugged, "I knew that I would be able to see you."

He tried not to show how much those words meant to him. He pointed to her necklace, "Nice necklace. Is it new?" He wanted to fish to see what she would say. "I see it has rubies and topazes in it."

She smiled, holding the necklace. "Yes, I just got it today. As you know my birthday is in April and Erick's is in November." His face fell. He couldn't believe his luck. Her eyes lit up and she laughed, "I didn't think about that, but so is yours."

He nodded, "The eighteenth. How about him?"

"The twelfth." She replied. She seemed to think about that, "What a coincidence."

"I'll say," He mumbled. "Well, I think that's amazing news about the job. We should celebrate tonight. I can pick you up when I get off work today. It will be about six o'clock. Does that work?"

"That would be great," she smiled. "I'll see you later."

"See you," He called, as she left his office.

He sunk down in his chair and opened up his desk drawer. He pulled the letter out from the corner of his desk. He read through it. It was time to make the next move. He was sure of it. He folded the letter and put it into his jacket pocket. He got up and left his office for another meeting. By the end of the evening she would know exactly how he felt and he could hope that she felt the same.

*****

Tiffany tried one more time to call Erick. She groaned in frustration, disconnecting the call. She didn't know why she couldn't get ahold of him. She heard a knock and she went to answer it. "I will be with you in a minute." She called, heading back to get her purse.

"I thought we could have a picnic today. If that's alright with you?"

She frowned, "It's been pretty cold. Are you sure about that?"

He snickered, "Where we're going it won't be cold. I promise."

She thought that was strange, but shrugged. "Whatever. I'm game if you are." She shut her hotel room door and headed with him down the elevator and out the hotel. They got to his car and she saw the picnic basket in the backseat. "It's been awhile since I've been on a picnic," I admitted.

"I think you'll be surprised by the location," he replied. Their eyes connected and he was smiling. She got into the car and he went around to the other side. The drive was quiet, but in a good way. When they turned the corner, she remembered how they had come down this same road a few days ago. She glanced at him and he was just smiling. She didn't bother mentioning it. When they pulled into the driveway, she knew that something was going on.

"What are we doing here?" She asked, staring up at the first house they had visited. A *Sold* sign was in front of it. "What's going on?"

He laughed, "You'll see."

They got out of the car and he grabbed the picnic basket. They then headed up to the front door. She watched as he unlocked the door with a set of keys. "What in the world?" She asked, entering the house.

He turned around, "I bought it."

Her jaw dropped, "Are you serious?"

He laughed, "I knew you would say that. I just fell in love with this house and decided that it was time to make the move. What do you think?"

"I think you are out of your mind." She replied, smacking him on the arm. "This is pretty cool, but sad. You got a house before me and I was the one looking."

He laughed, "I'm sorry, but I didn't want to pass it up."

She had to admit she was a little jealous, but she was also thrilled for him. "Congrats Scott," she leaned up to kiss his cheek, but he turned his head so that her lips were touching his. The kiss lingered for a moment, until she realized what was happening. "Scott..." she said, touching her lips.

"Tiffany, listen to me." He said. He took his hand to her waist and she slowly pulled away.

"I'm getting married," she quickly said, moving backwards.

"He hasn't even called you." He argued.

She glared at him. "He's sent me flowers and a necklace to show me that he is thinking about me. That's all I need."

He moved to her, "Tiffany, I bought you those things." He said.

She opened her mouth, but no words came out. She shook her head, "You're lying. His birthstone..."

"Is my birthstone. You said it yourself. I know your favorite flower. Go with your heart. Do you honestly think I'm making this up?"

She didn't know what to believe. She was going to be Erick's wife and this wasn't supposed to happen like this. "I am getting married," she spoke again.

"To the wrong man," he replied.

"Stop it!" She yelled. "You are my best friend and nothing will ever happen between us."

"Why not? Are you that scared?" He asked, intently staring at her.

"Why are you doing this? I know those gifts came from Erick." She looked away from him, feeling tears stinging the back of her eyes. "Take me home."

"Tiffany, don't....talk to me."

She shook her head, "Take me home." She spoke again. She turned from him and ran from the house. She couldn't let him get to her. She knew the truth and that's what mattered.

*****

"Tiffany, won't you please hear me out." Scott said for the hundredth time. "I wouldn't lie to you."

She couldn't stay in that car and listen to him. Nothing seemed real. She reached for her door handle. "Don't call me," she said, with anger in her voice.

Pain was etched on his face. He pulled something from his jacket pocket and placed it in her hand. "Just read it. Please."

She closed her hand on the letter. She anticipated, she would just throw it away, but she didn't say that. "Goodnight," she replied, jumping out of the car and heading into the hotel.

The moment she got inside, she felt the tears fall. She got into the elevator, feeling her body shaking from the tears. When she got out of the elevator, she walked to her room. She opened the door and fell to the bed.

She looked at the folded piece of paper and thought about just throwing it away. Instead, she opened it up and started to read. The more she read the worse she felt. She covered her mouth. The fact that he felt that was shocking to her, but it didn't change the fact that she wasn't available. As she got up, she threw the note into the wastebasket. She heard her cellphone ringing and she grabbed it from her pocket. She sighed with relief, seeing Erick's name across the screen.

"Hello."

"Hey, babe. It's been awhile."

She wanted to argue that that was his fault, but she didn't have the energy. "You have no idea how much I needed to hear your voice." She said, falling back down on the bed.

"I'm sorry I have been out of touch. It's been crazy, but I did get your messages." She held onto his words. It would be a relief to hear him talk about the gifts that he got her. "I must admit, I'm a little confused. What flowers and necklace are you referring to?"

A gasp escaped her lips. This couldn't be. "Um…never mind, I was mistaken." She said, dumbfounded.

"Oh…" he snickered.

She felt a weight in her chest, but tried to get over it. "I got a job today."

There was a long pause, before he spoke again. "You did? There's actually something that I need to tell you."

"I'm listening."

"There has been a change of plans. I was offered a better position if I stay here. It equals more money and more responsibilities. In the long run I can't pass it up."

"You didn't call me. This would be news that you should have told me before I went and got another job."

"I know, baby, but I just found out and I couldn't let you know earlier. It wasn't finalized. Just tell the place that hired you that you're fiancé is staying in New York. They'll understand."

She couldn't find the words to express how upset she was. "I won't understand. This job is giving me opportunities that I don't want to pass up. I love you, but..." her words dropped off.

"What are you trying to say?"

"We barely know each other. You are obviously more wrapped up in your job than I could ever compete with."

"That's not true," he argued.

"Yes...it is." She continued, "It would never work out."

"But..."

"I will mail you the ring back. Good luck and I wish you every bit of happiness."

"Tiffany, don't..." he started, saying the same words that Scott had spoken. She hung up the phone, feeling relief.

She looked at her ring and pulled it off her finger. She placed it on the dresser and went back to the wastebasket. She picked up the letter and reread it. She knew that Scott was someone that could handle a mixture of being with her and working. She grabbed her purse and headed to the door. She needed to talk to him and she hoped there was a cab around. When she opened the door, she nearly ran right into him. "I, couldn't just leave..." he began, before he could go on she wrapped her hand around his neck and pulled him close to her. Their lips connected and she melted into him. His tongue ran along hers and she pulled from him.

"I'm sorry," she spoke, grabbing his hand and pulling him into the hotel room. "I love you," she spoke, pulling him back to her and wrapping her arms around him. They could talk later. The only thing that mattered to her was showing him how much she cared for him and she would show him that the rest of her life.

****

Lost Love

Although Chase had broken up with her 2 years earlier, Liv hoped for a reconciliation. Chase had long since moved on, while Liv, a hair stylist, never went out on a single date. When they first broke up, Chase wasn't sure that he made the right decision.

As time wore on, however, his feelings for Liv were quickly fading. Conversely, Liv's feelings were getting stronger for Chase, despite his snubs.

Liv, a seasoned employee at Salon54, first laid eyes on Chase when he came in to get his haircut. Liv and her friends were swooning over this six-foot-two brunette who walked in with a confident smirk. He knew he was hot.

Liv thought he was the hottest guy she has ever seen but felt that he was "out of her league." Chase was a partner in a large law firm who played polo, was a member of a posh country club, and who traveled all over the world. Of course she didn't know that at the time, but his appearance and attitude ended up perfectly matching his background. No surprise there.

Liv came from a blue-collar family, whose father was a construction worker. Her mother was a stay-at-home mom, but worked part-time as a manicurist in the basement of their modest Seattle home.

While in high school, Liv excelled in math and science, but her family was unable to afford sending her to college. She wanted to become an engineer, but her dreams were dashed when her father lost his job.

Liv had to go to work to help support the family, and in her spare time, she decided to go to cosmetology school. She paid for her beauty school tuition out of the money she made from working at the local pet shop, and after about a year, she passed the state boards to become a licensed cosmetologist.

On Liv's 30th birthday, her friends took her out to a popular nightclub to celebrate. Although she met a few guys that sparked her interest, all she could think about was Chase. She was hoping that he would make a second appointment for a haircut and return to the salon.

As luck would have it, Chase returned to the salon a couple months later, and to Liv's complete surprise, he asked her out. Their first date took them to Chase's country club, where Liv met his friends.

Chase was 10 years older than Liv, although he acted and looked much younger. Even though he acted youthful and vibrant, his friends seemed boring and arrogant. Despite her dislike for his friends, Liv quickly fell in love with Chase. He treated her well, and even offered to pay for her to go back to college.

The couple soon settled into a mundane dating routine, and although Liv was still happy, she could sense that Chase was losing interest in her. He seemed irritated and distant with her, and started going out a few times a week.

Most of Chase's family members liked Liv, however, his mother never warmed up to her. She never thought that Liv was good enough for her son, but remained cordial to her.

Chase's mother, Vera, on more than one occasion, tried introducing her son to various women. These women were all professionals, and a few were attorneys, just like her son.

Chase's father, Jack, also an attorney, stayed out of his wife's matchmaking schemes, as he was in his own little world, with a mistress of his own and a huge drinking problem.

Chase didn't invite Liv to his grandmother's birthday party, and when he arrived, he was greeted at the door by one of the most beautiful women he'd ever seen. He never saw her before, and wondered who she was there with. Little did he know, his mother invited her in an attempt to get him interested in someone other than Liv.

Her plan worked. Chase and the other women, whose name was Chelsea, hit it off almost instantly. He couldn't stop looking at her, and was intrigued by her New York accent.

Chelsea worked as an entertainment attorney, who represented a number of big name sports and music personalities. She even invited Chase to a sporting event which had been sold out for weeks.

Even though Chase had no intentions of breaking up with Liv, he could no longer ignore his feelings for Chelsea. They soon started having lunch dates at 5 star hotels, and even managed to plan a getaway weekend to the Poconos.

When Chase started becoming increasingly distant from Liv, she started to suspect the worst. By this time, Chelsea was pressuring Chase for a commitment. Although they've only been seeing each other for about a month, their relationship was growing more and more intense.

The sex was amazing, and Chase never experienced anything like it before. Chelsea was willing to try new things in bed, and seemed to want sex multiple times a day. Liv, by contrast, was rather modest, and her sexual appetite was diminished by her escalating depression, and the side effects from the medication she was taking.

As the months passed, Liv was getting ready to go to Florida for a hair show. She and Chase were drifting further and further apart, but they still managed to maintain a dim spark of excitement between them. On the evening before she was schedule to leave for her trip, Liv and Chase went out for a romantic dinner, and then came home and spent the next three hours making love.

After their love fest, Chase turned over and went to sleep. Liv, the eternal romantic, want to cuddle, but Chase rebuffed her advances. The next morning, Chase drove Liv to the airport, and he couldn't help but feel profound relief. He would now be able to spend the next week with his new "friend," Chelsea, and called her as soon as Liv boarded the plane.

For almost the entire week that Liv was on her business trip, Chase stayed with Chelsea at her downtown apartment. The couple enjoyed cooking dinner together and waking up next to each other. Chase didn't know how he would tell Liv that he no longer loved her, and he even wished that she would stay in Florida for the long-term.

He was not responsive to her text messages, and only took her phone calls sporadically during that entire week. The week flew by quickly, and before he knew it, Chase found himself at the airport once again, but only this time, he was picking Liv up. She was elated to see him, but he cringed when they hugged.

Liv sensed that something was wrong, and was starting to worry. Chase told her that he was tired because he spent the entire week working on a brief for an upcoming legal case.

The couple trudged through the holidays together, but as Valentine's Day approached, Chase could no longer suppress he desire to be with Chelsea. Although he knew that Valentine's week was not the most appropriate time to break up with Liv, he felt it was necessary, because he wanted to spend Valentine's Day with Chelsea.

He didn't bother with formalities, and simply blurted it out. He told Liv that he was no longer happy with her, but didn't volunteer any information about his other woman. He further explained that he just needed time to be "by himself," and that "maybe" he would come to his senses and come back home to be with her. After Liv pressed him for answers, he finally came clean about Chelsea.

After hearing the news, Liv broke down, and didn't think she would be able to function at work the next day. Of course, Chase told her that he didn't mean for it to happen, but when he met Chelsea, an instant connection was made. He didn't really want to divulge so much information about how he felt about Chelsea, but he felt that unless he "drove his point home," Liv wouldn't take him seriously.

Liv was blindsided by the breakup. She tried to keep busy with work and going out with friends, but she couldn't shake the despair she felt. Although she was asked out on dates, she always declined.

In Liv's eyes, nobody would ever hold a candle to Chase, and she had no desire to date anyone because she knew it would never progress into anything further. In the meantime, Chase and Chelsea were seen around town at various restaurants and social events.

On one occasion, Liv caught a glimpse of the couple getting out of a cab. This almost pushed her over the edge, but she managed to hold onto her dignity. After three years passed, Liv's feelings for Chase were still as intense as they were when they first started dated. Chase's feelings for Liv, on the other hand, were almost non-existent. Sure he had fond memories of their time together, but never really felt as though Liv was his soul mate.

Liv eventually started seeing a counselor because she was not bouncing back from the breakup. Her sleep pattern was disrupted, her diet was poor, and she stopped socializing altogether. The only social stimulation she got was when she went to work, and even there, her social interactions were severely limited.

The counselor was worried for his patient's safety, and feared that she was spiraling into a deep, dark depression. Liv was eventually referred to a psychiatrist, who adjusted her medication and sent her on her way. When the medication kicked in after a few weeks, Liv's mood brightened, and she started considering dating again.

Liv met a nice guy at the gym, and when he asked her out for coffee, she felt flattered. Like Chase, Jason was older, distinguished and well-educated. Their coffee date was pleasant, but according to Liv, there was no spark.

When Jason asked her out for dinner, Liv hesitated, but decided to give him another chance. She was very critical of other men, but hoped that she would once again, find love. Jason took Liv to dinner and a play, and as the date was coming to a close, Jason leaned in for a kiss.

Liv had no intentions of kissing him, and in fact, she had no intentions of ever seeing him again. All she could think about was Chase. Three years have passed, and still, her love was as strong as ever. Liv's co-workers were worried about her, and when she had too much to drink one night and drunk dialed Chase, they really became concerned. Fortunately she hung up before he answered the phone, but her number showed up on his caller ID.

Chase was curious to find out what Liv wanted. His relationship with Chelsea was starting to cool, and lately, he started thinking about how much Liv loved him when they were together. He hesitated at first, but after a couple days, Chase returned Liv's call.

You could have knocked her over with a feather when she saw Chase's number come up on her caller ID. She was shaking as she answered the phone, and as soon as she heard his voice, she broke down sobbing.

Something stirred in Chase's heart, because he too, felt tears welling up in his eyes. Their phone call was brief, and in fact, it lasted only seconds, because Chelsea walked into the room just as Liv answered. Chase took this as a sign.

Liv knew that Chase still felt a connection to her. She quickly put that phone call out of her mind, and tried to focus on her job. She went on a few more dates, and much to her surprise, Liv found a guy with whom she clicked with.

Her friend introduced her to an accountant who was from the same town that Liv was from. In fact, they lived within a few blocks of each other when they were teenagers, but they went to different schools. He went to a private, all-boys school, and Liv went to a public school.

At first, the relationship progressed slowly, but after a few months, Liv started developing strong feelings for her new friend, whose name was Ben. He took Liv to meet his family in Florida, and they absolutely loved her. Unlike Chase's mother, Vera, Ben's mother, Patty, felt that they were the perfect couple.

As their relationship grew stronger, Liv's feelings for Chase were becoming distant memories. In fact, days went by where she didn't even think about Chase at all. Chase, on the other hand, couldn't get Liv out of his mind. His relationship with Chelsea was hanging by a thread, and he yearned for the relationship he once shared with Liv.

He was starting to realize that breaking up with her was a mistake, and he hoped that she was not involved with another man. Chase finally raised enough courage to call Liv back, and when she answered, his heart stopped. He almost hung up, but was able to whisper out a weak, "Hi Liv, how are you?" Liv was gracious and warm, and replied, "Hi, Chase, it's nice to hear from you."

The conversation was strained and awkward, but in Chase's mind, the ice had been broken. He was certain that he could get back into Liv's good graces once again, so that they could pick up where they left off. Their conversation consisted solely of small talk, and neither one asked about the other's personal life.

Liv almost felt sick to her stomach when she heard Chase's voice, because it brought back the painful memories of their breakup. She was grateful that she had Ben, because he filled the void that Chase left. When she told Ben that Chase called, he became suspicious. Why would Chase call Liv after three years apart? Did Liv initiate the first call, he wondered? Liv finally confessed to Ben that she did, indeed, "drunk dial" Chase days before.

It seemed that now, the tables were turned. Chase was the one who was pining away for Liv, while Liv, on the other hand, was blissfully "in like" with someone else. It never occurred to Chase that Liv would move on and start a new life with someone else. He also felt that Liv was his "ace in the hole," in case his relationship with Chelsea didn't work out. Would he and Liv ever reconcile, he wondered?

Even though Liv was happy with Ben, she couldn't get Chase out of her mind, and wanted to connect with him again, just to find out more about his relationship status with Chelsea.

Liv felt a twinge of guilt for thinking about calling Chase because Ben had been so good to her. She didn't want to be shady or go behind his back, so she talked to him about her intentions.

Liv felt that she needed to get Chase out of her system once and for all before she would be able to move forward with her relationship with Ben. A total commitment to Ben was out of the question, in Liv's mind, unless she was completely over Chase.

Ben agreed that Liv needed to get Chase out of her system before they could take the next step in their relationship, so he encouraged Liv to make the phone call. Feeling better now that she confessed her feelings to Ben about Chase, Liv picked up her phone and dialed Chase's number.

He answered on the first ring, and couldn't believe his good fortune that Liv was calling him. "I want to see you," Liv said, as soon as Chase answered the phone.

Chase was shocked, but elated. By this time, he and Chelsea were barely speaking, and she was spending more and more time away from the apartment that they shared since the beginning of their relationship.

Liv and Chase planned to go out for dinner so that could talk. Both were excited, anxious, but uncertain about a future together. When Liv saw Chase for the first time in three years, she was surprised that her heart wasn't racing, and that she did not have butterflies in her stomach.

Although it was nice to see Chase, that intense spark of passion and love was not there. Chase, on the other hand, could barely contain his emotions, and started to cry when they hugged.

He apologized to Liv for hurting her, but she was unfazed. The cold and uncaring manner in which he "dumped" Liv always bothered

Chase, but he never had the opportunity to tell Liv how he felt. They talked about Chase's relationship with Chelsea, and how it started out so intensely, but then, over time, seemed to have burned itself out.

Liv listened quietly as Chase spoke about how Chelsea was a workaholic, and how she never cooked a meal for him in three years. Not only didn't she cook, she never cleaned either. Chase finally hired a cleaning service to come in twice a month to tidy up, but he wished that Chelsea was a little more domesticated.

She wasn't into the "housewife" thing, and she certainly didn't have any maternal instincts either. Liv couldn't help but feel a twinge of satisfaction while Chase was droning on about his faltering relationship with Chelsea. Chase was the type of guy who enjoyed home-cooked meals, who liked a clean home, and who wanted to start a family someday.

Liv wanted to start a family too, but it was becoming more apparent to Liv, that instead of wanting to start a family with Chase, she wanted to start one with Ben. Throughout the entire dinner, Chase talked about himself and his relationship with Chelsea. He didn't ask Liv what was going on in her life until it was almost time for them to leave.

Chase was certain that Liv had been waiting around for him to come back all this time, and was profoundly disappointed when Liv told him that she had met someone else. What made Chase feel even worse was when Liv told him that she was falling in love with Ben. Chase asked, "how could you have fallen out of love with me?" Liv replied, "It took a long time, but I finally found someone who appreciates me, embraces me for who I am, and whose family loves me." On one hand, Chase was happy for Liv, but on the other hand, he was jealous, hurt and angry.

How could he have let Liv go? He knew what a great woman she was, but he let his mother's silly opinion of Liv get in the way. Chase now realizes that Liv was the "one that got away," and his hopes of finding his one true love have been dashed.

As their dinner date was ending, Chase felt that he had lost Liv forever. He decided to swallow his pride and beg Liv for another chance. He realized the error of his ways, and vowed that if she would give him another chance, he would do everything in his power to make her the happiest women alive.

Although tempting, Liv gently declined. Her feelings for Chase had changed, and she knew that she would never be able to love him like she once had. Chase wouldn't let up on his request for another chance, and Liv, who kept politely turning him down, was getting increasingly aggravated by his persistence. Liv once thought that the sun rose and set on Chase, but now, she was beginning to see his true colors emerge.

Chase had always been on the arrogant side, and was accustomed to getting his way all the time. He was spoiled as a child, and always seemed to have the upper hand when it came to relationships. If he didn't get what he wanted, he became pushy, overbearing and selfish.

Chase was sure that if he kissed Liv, that old spark would re-ignite in her soul. Not only did Liv turn away from Chase's attempt at a kiss, she was repelled by it. He no longer had the same effect on her, and in fact, she wished that she could have snapped her fingers to bring her back home to Ben. She felt safe with Ben because he was so genuine and kind. There was not an arrogant or selfish bone in his body.

Liv always lived on the edge with Chase, and always questioned his feelings for her. She knows that Ben is in love with her, and only her. He is not on the lookout for someone better, or for someone who is on the same level as he is educationally. Even though Liv doesn't have a college education, she is extremely bright, quick witted, wise and perceptive. Qualities that Chase never saw in her.

He criticized Liv because of the way she spoke and because she never attended college. He wanted to pay for her college education so that she could "better herself," however, Liv believes that he only wanted her to go to college because he was concerned that she wasn't "scholarly" enough, and that it didn't look good for him to be with an "uneducated" woman.

Just to make sure that Chase was completely out of her system, Liv relented and kissed him. The kiss soon became more intense, and Liv could sense that Chase was getting overly enthusiastic. Since she wasn't feeling the same way, she retreated. She now knew, for sure, that Chase wasn't the man for her. When she kissed Ben, passion stirs inside her, but when she kissed Chase, she felt nothing.

Although Liv felt guilty about kissing Chase, because she knew it would hurt Ben, she just had to know for sure if the excitement, love and passion were still there. They were for Chase, but not for Liv. It was then and there, that she decided to say good-bye, once and for all. Liv would never turn back, and would finally close that chapter in her life.

After a year had gone by, Liv and Ben started planning their wedding. They were now totally committed to each other, and were living together. Liv quit her job as a hair stylist, and was now working for Ben. This allowed them to spend all day together, which they cherished. Some couples enjoy the time they spend away from each other while they are both at their respective jobs, but for Liv and Ben, working together in the same office works well for them. In addition to being soul mates, they are best friends, and can let their respective guards down when they are together. Although Ben is technically Liv's boss, he never plays that card. He is also careful to never show favoritism to Liv in front of his other employees. He treats everyone with respect, and no one is treated better than anyone else. Many of Ben's employees have been with his for years, which is a true testament to his character. Liv is proud to be his life partner, both personally and professionally.

Liv was getting excited for her wedding, and before the big day, members of her bridal party gave her a bachelorette party. Liv almost forgot what it was like to have a good time with her friends, because the last time they all went out together, Liv was in a funk over Chase. She is grateful that her friends saw her through her ordeal, and is honored to have them be a part of her wedding day. The celebration started off at a neighborhood bar where the ladies indulged in a few tropical drinks, then it was off to Liv's favorite restaurant. The night was exciting and fun, and Liv couldn't remember when she had such a fun time with her friends. The merriment came to a screeching halt in the blink of an eye, however. While the ladies were enjoying their dinner and each other's company, a familiar figure walked through the door. It was none other than Chase. He was accompanied by an older woman, who Liv later recognized as his mother, Vera. The two looked solemn as they were seated at their table, and barely spoke to one another while they dined.

Chase and his mother hadn't yet noticed that Liv was at the restaurant, and Liv wanted it to stay that way. She didn't want anything casting a pall over her special evening, but when she had to go to the bathroom, she wondered how she'd sneak past their table without her cover being blown. After thinking about it, she realized that she didn't care if they saw her or not. She didn't owe either one of them anything and didn't even feel obligated to greet them. Liv and her entourage made a beeline for the bathroom, but not before Chase's mother noticed them. "Isn't that Liv?" she asked.

Chase was stunned and took this as another opportunity to try and win her back. It's fate, he thought. Yes, it was fate, but not in the way that Chase had hoped for. He stalked the bathroom door and waiting for Liv to come out. When she did, he greeted her with a hug. Liv tried to be personable, but again, she couldn't hide her disdain for Chase.

Liv and Chase ended up having a brief conversation. Liv was more than happy to tell Chase about her impending nuptials to Ben. She then learned why Chase and his mother looked so stone-faced when they walked into the restaurant.

It turned out that Chase was the one who was now battling severe depression ever since Liv didn't return his affections the last time they had dinner together. In fact, his depression got so bad that he had to give up his law practice and move in with his mother.

This was the first night he had been out in public in months. His relationship with Chelsea had long since fell apart, and he was having a hard time re-building his life. Liv felt bad for Chase, and now wondered if his mother felt any remorse for sticking her nose in their business by setting him up with Chelsea.

Liv and Ben were married in a beautiful ceremony, and now have an adorable baby girl. Chase is still living with his mother, and has let his law license expire. He did get a job working as a handyman in the neighborhood, however, and Liv has since shown pity on him and hired him to install a white picket fence around her and Ben's sprawling new home.

****

Legal Affairs

Jennifer was ecstatic when she left her job interview because she knew she impressed Trevor, the charismatic, handsome lawyer with whom's firm she was seeking employment with.

"I see that you've worked as a paralegal for a couple years," Trevor commented after reading Jennifers's resume.

"Yes, I was hired right out of college by the law firm that represented my father when he owned some commercial property," Jennifer replied.

While she was trying to pay attention to his words, Jennifer was mesmerized by Trevor's striking blue eyes and dazzling smile. She also felt a twinge of excitement when she noticed that the debonair attorney wasn't wearing a wedding ring.

Trevor was brilliant, and even though he was a partner in a prestigious law firm, he was only 25 years old. He graduated college very early and finished law school before most of his classmates even completed high school.

"Where do you see yourself professionally in the next five years?" Jennifer was unprepared to answer this question, and while she tried her best to sound creative and profound, she worried that she came off silly and trite.

"I would like to be working for a well-established law firm where I could further my knowledge of the legal system as it pertains to corporate law and international economics," she sputtered.

Jennifer was so mortified by her reply that she could literally feel her face getting red and hot. She wished that she would have prepared for the interview more, but it was too late now, she thought.

Trevor seemed to be impressed with everything Jennifer had to say, and even more so with the tight, low-cut blouse she was wearing. Jennifer, or Jen, as she liked to be called, thought about dressing conservatively, but decided to be a bit more daring.

"Why should I hire you?" Again, Jen wasn't prepared to answer this question, but quickly came up with a clever answer that even she was impressed with. "This is my dream job.

Some of the other applicants might have more experience or better credentials than I do, but after a couple of months or so, I'll have those same credentials, and I'll also have the passion that those other applicants lack," Jen replied.

The rest of the interview went well and Trevor told Jennifer that he would be in touch. Jen's post-interview euphoria was short-lived because days went by with no phone call from the hunky legal eagle.

Finally, after about two weeks he called and left a message on her cell. "Hi, Jennifer, this is Trevor Parker from the law firm and I'm calling to see if you are still interested in the job, and if you are, please call me back."

Jennifer didn't want to seem desperate, so she waited a respectable 2 hours before she returned his phone call. She was so nervous, she could barely catch her breath, and for a minute, she thought about hanging up.

Trevor's secretary answered on the second ring and promptly transferred Jen over to his extension. "Trevor Parker speaking, may I help you?" Jennifer's heart skipped a beat but she managed to keep her cool. "Hello, Mr. Parker, this is Jennifer Adams returning your call."

Trevor responded, "Hey, Jennifer, thanks for calling back, and please, call me Trevor."

"Very well, Trevor!"

"Jennifer, I would like to offer you the paralegal position."

"Thank you, I accept," Jen replied.

"I'm a laid-back type of boss, so if you don't mind, why don't we discuss the details of the job over coffee at the corner cafe instead of at the office?"

Jen replied, "That would be great, I love that little cafe, it's so quaint."

Trevor responded, "Great, how does Thursday at 11:00 sound?"

"It sounds perfect," Jen said.

"Fantastic, I'll see you then!" replied Trevor.

Jennifer called everyone she knew to tell them about her new job. Actually it wasn't so much the job she was gushing over as it was her new boss, Trevor. She couldn't believe her good luck.

She never thought she would find a job this quick, and only in her wildest dream did she ever think that she would be working for someone who looked like Trevor. Not only was he gorgeous, he seemed very kind, easy to get along with and super funny.

Jen couldn't decide on what to wear for her meeting with Trevor, so she decided to buy something new. She really wasn't in a position to be buying new clothes, but this was a special occasion.

At the store, Jennifer tried on at least a dozen outfits but couldn't make up her mind. She finally decided on a tight-fitting black dress that was professional enough for a business meeting but seductive enough, she thought, to get Trevor's attention.

When Thursday finally rolled around, Jen was beside herself with excitement. She felt confident in how she looked, but she was so nervous that she forgot to put on lipstick.

Jen never goes out of the house without lipstick, but by the time she realized that she had forgotten to put it on, it was too late to turn back and go home. Instead, she ran into the closest drug store and bought a cheap tube.

Not only did she purchase the lipstick, she also purchased a box of condoms, just in case. Jen has never slept with someone after only meeting them once, but she had a feeling about how her meeting with Trevor was going to go.

Sure, this was a business meeting of sorts, but she felt such a connection to Trevor and she knew that it was reciprocated. She was very hot to trot for her new boss and wanted to be prepared in the event that things heated up after their meeting.

Trevor arrived early to the cafe and took the liberty of ordering two large coffees and a couple blueberry scones. Soon after, Jennifer arrived, confident in her appearance, thanks to her new lipstick purchase.

Trevor, the gallant gentlemen that he is, stood up and pulled out her chair. After exchanging pleasantries, they discussed the job.

Trevor offered Jen almost twice as much as she was making at her last job, and she wouldn't be working weekends or holidays either. "How does 4 weeks vacation sound?"

Jen's last job only allowed for a one week vacation after being on the job for a year, and having four weeks vacation was the icing on the cake. "It almost sounds too good to be true," she replied.

After Trevor and Jen were finished discussing the details of the job, their conversation quickly turned personal. They found out that they had mutual friends and that they once even worked for the same company.

After feeling more comfortable with one another, Trevor asked Jen if she would like to join him for dinner at his home.

He lived only a few blocks from the cafe, and because he was a gourmet cook, he was looking forward to preparing his new employee the best meal of her life. Feeding her, however, wasn't the only thing on his agenda.

Trevor was instantly attracted to Jennifer the moment he first saw her. The sexual chemistry was obvious, which is why Jen purchased the condoms at the drug store when she bought her lipstick.

"Your home is spectacular," Jen told Trevor.

"Thank you, Jen. I bought it from one of the partners of the law firm who retired to Florida about a year ago."

Before the couple made their way into the kitchen to start dinner, they started kissing as soon as they got into the house.

Jennifer vowed that if she ever "married rich," she would give her parents enough money so that their lives would change for the better.

She would pay all their bills, buy them a new home and make sure that they never worried about money again.

Trevor shook his head moving closer to her and putting his hands on her blouse. "We're being irrational. Just go for it. He ripped the shirt from her body and it fell to the floor. His lips went to her neck, while her hands went to his shirt, removing it from the confinement of his dress pants.

She started off tediously undoing button after button, but then knew that she needed to move the show on the road. She busted open his shirt, the way that he had busted open hers.

Her hands trailed down his chest, while he continued to kiss her neck. She arched her back, sighing against his kisses. His hands went behind her back, as he slowly removed her bra. Her breasts pressed hard against his bare chest.

Her hands went to his pants and she quickly removed them. They fell to the floor and he kicked them off. Then his hands went to his boxers and she drug them down his legs, while his hands caressed her nipples. She eyed his manhood, salivating at the sight.

His hands slowly slid down her stomach and then wrapped around her back. He undid the zipper to her skirt and it fell to the floor.

His hands went to her panties and he looped his fingers through them, tugging them off of her body. Before she had time to comprehend the next move, she felt him lifting her into his arms and laying her down on the floor.

Their lips met, his tongue dipping inside her mouth. As their tongues clashed together, his hands continued to massage her breasts, gently feeling each part of her sensitive skin.

As he was about to enter her, he pulled back. "Damn, I don't have a condom," he groaned, starting to regress.

"It's your lucky day, because I have one," Jen coyly replied. She had almost forgotten that she bought them earlier.

She wrapped her arms around him and pulled him closer to her. "Ugh..." she groaned, arching her back, but not breaking from the kiss.

As each thrust turned harder, she was forced to part from the kiss. "Ugh...Oh God...yes..." she whimpered, barely able to get the words out, it felt so good.

As one arm continued being wrapped around him, her other arm fell down to her side and she tried desperately to grab anything to hold onto, finally choosing for a leg to his chair. Her hips bucked against his.

He pressed up against her, with a hunger that she never endured. "Oh God...yes...yes..." he cried, pressing harder to her core.

"Wow..." she sighed, closing her eyes and just lying there. As she was focusing on her next move, she felt hands on her legs, parting her ever so softly.

Then it was over and she was fighting disappointment, until she felt something else. She tried to control her breathing, as she felt his tongue exploring every inch of her body.

She felt the smoothness of his moves and she sighed against his deep and masculine movements. "Hm...hmmm...hm..." she signed, her body gliding against the intensity.

As his tongue was seeking out each crevice that she could provide, she felt her body begin to shake with desire.

As his tongue slowly weaved its way out of her mouth, she dropped her hands from his head. She closed her eyes and took in deep and slow breaths. She felt him easing his way back up her. Her eyes opened and she stared at him. She only saw desire and nothing else.

He wrapped his hand around her neck and pulled her into a breathless kiss. His tongue circling around hers. He pulled from the kiss, bringing his mouth down to her flesh of her neck. She could barely keep up, as she was fighting exhaustion.

She closed her eyes and tried to focus on his intimate paths around her skin. Between kisses, she heard his words. "God, you're sexy!" She could relish in that forever.

When she felt him retracting, she heaved a sigh. He fell off of her and she could hear the restlessness that he felt. "Wow..." he mumbled, as they both just laid there and tried to catch their breath.

After their rendevous, Trevor led Jennifer into the kitchen while he prepared their dinner. Not only was Jennifer impressed by is sexual prowess, she was also floored by his cooking skills. "Where in the world did you learn how to cook like this?"

Trevor replied, "Believe it or not, I studied in Paris at the Cordon Bleu after graduating from law school." He went on to say, "I had dreams of owning my own restaurant for as long as I can remember."

The dinner was extraordinary, and Jennifer couldn't believe her good luck. What more could she ask for? She was just offered a great-paying job, her laywer boss was gorgeous and very interested in her, he was a great lover and an amazing cook.

Jennifer wouldn't starting her job at Trevor's law firm for two more weeks, and during this time, she was hoping that she would be able to spend more time with him to get to know him better.

After they finished dinner and chatted for a while longer, it was time for Jen to leave. Trevor was leaving for a business trip in the morning and would need to leave for the airport very early.

The couple kissed good-bye and Trevor assured Jen that he would call her when he settled into his hotel room the next day.

Jennifer couldn't think about anything but Trevor. He's the best lover she'd ever had, and even though they only knew each other for a day or so, she felt that she was falling in love with him.

Jen believed in love at first sight, and when she called her mother to tell her that she's met the man of her dreams, her mother was not as thrilled as Jen hoped she would be.

"What do you know about this guy?" Jen replied, "I know that he's a rich, gorgeous lawyer who makes a mean chateaubriand steak."

Jennifer's mother had an uneasy feeling about the whole thing, but she tried to sound happy and encouraging.

Jen waited for Trevor to call her when he got to the hotel the next day. When it got to be 10pm, she got concerned, not because she didn't think he would call, but because she feared that something may have happened to him. Since Jennifer didn't have Trevor's cellphone number, she was unable to call him to make sure he was alright.

Trevor never called that night, and in fact, Jen never heard from him at all. After two weeks went by, it was time for Jen to start her new job at Trevor's law firm.

When Jennifer arrived at the office, the receptionist let Trevor know that Jennifer was waiting to see him. When Trevor walked into the lobby, Jennifer could barely catch her breath.

She was expecting a robust welcome from her new boss in light of their wild night of passionate sex, but instead, he greeted her with a curt, "Good morning Ms. Adams. Welcome to the law firm." He barely looked at her.

Trevor acted like he didn't even know Jen, and because of this, she felt like walking out the door. She didn't even want to start her new job. How could he treat her like this, she wondered. She wondered if she'd said something to offend him or if he was turned off by her passion.

Jennifer asked Trevor how his business trip was and he replied with a cold, "Very well, thank you." Jen was shocked by his attitude and was even starting to feel a little scared.

Although she thought of quitting, she decided to make the best out of the job. It paid well, it was close to her home and the benefits were excellent. Jennifer was going to ask Trevor what his problem was and why he was treating her so poorly, but she decided to just let it go.

She was simply going to chalk up the experience with Trevor as a one-night stand. She's had them before where the guy never called her, so why should this time be any different. It was just weird because this time, the guy was going to be her new boss.

After a couple days, Jen was starting to settle into her new job, and despite all the drama with Trevor, she was actually starting to feel comfortable. She got along with the other lawyers and paralegals, and while Trevor still treated her like a stranger, he was very professional towards her.

It wasn't until about a month later that Jen found out that Trevor's great grandfather started the law firm many years ago and than his grandfather and father had also been partners. The firm was steeped in tradition and professionalism, and Trevor intended to keep it that way.

Jennifer also treated Trevor with respect and never held his icy attitude towards her against him. As time went by, Trevor started to warm up. One day, he asked Jennifer to come into his office.

She didn't think anything of it and assumed it was to talk about a case she was working on. Jen enjoyed working on this particular case because she got to know the client and his wife very well. They were extremely nice, and they even told Trevor how highly they thought of Jennifer. This is exactly what he needed to hear.

Trevor held his law firm in very high regard because it was so steeped in tradition. He only employed those who he considered loyal, and who wouldn't "crack" under the pressures of working for him.

Doing what he did to Jennifer was somewhat of a test to determine if she had what it took to still do her job despite extenuating circumstances. He fully expected her to quit or not even show up on the first day of her job because he failed to call her after their sexual encounter.

After Jen proved that she could maintain her professionalism and even excel at her job in spite of what happened, proved to Trevor that she was the type of employee that he wanted at his law firm.

Trevor finally decided that he had to come clean. "I had to do what I did to prove to myself that you were right for the law firm."

He also said, "You see, Jen, I just wanted to make sure that you would still be able to perform your job in spite of adverse circumstances."

Jennifer replied, "I actually cared for you, and for me, it was more than just a one night stand."

Trevor responded, "I had feelings for you as well and even though I wanted so badly to call you when I got to the hotel, I just couldn't."

Trevor further explained that the law firm was almost "sacred" to him and he had to do everything in his power to ensure that the employees were dedicated and that they would not quit just "because."

While Jennifer thought his tactics were unethical, in a way, she understood why he did what he did. A couple of paralegals and attorneys quit abruptly at her last job, leaving the clients in the lurch. Because they quit so suddenly, cases were delayed, which often caused financial hardships for the litigants.

Trevor and the other partners in the law firm always saw to it that their clients were treated with the utmost respect and that their legal cases were handled as quickly and efficiently as possible.

Trevor now knew that Jen was "true blue" and dedicated to the law firm. She had a strong work ethic and her legal skills were an asset to the company. Once Trevor explained the reason behind his behavior, the couple hugged. Jen said, "I'm so glad you finally explained yourself."

She further said, "I don't think what you did to me was right, but I'm hoping that maybe we can start over, now that I "proved" myself to you." Trevor sheepishly replied, "I would love it."

The couple took it slowly and were very discreet around the office. They didn't want anyone to know about their relationship. After a few months, Jen and Trevor declared their love for one another and decided to get engaged.

Jen eventually applied to law school and was accepted. When she graduates and passes the bar exam, she'll become a partner in the law firm that she almost stopped working for.

****

The Billionaire's Secret

Amelia Randolph was fuming. Her grandmother was sick again, and it had to be the water. She paced the room in the hospital where she watched her grandmother sleeping. Nothing had been right in a long time, not since that ass, Jacob Montgomery had installed that new water filtration equipment.

She'd had her suspicions for a long time, but then they tested it, and she knew she had to be right. She had called, prodded and attacked everyone she could. It wasn't that she couldn't be a lady, she could. Her grandmother was the most important person to her and there was no way she could just stand idly by and wait for things to get worse.

Friday she would get her chance, until then she was doing her best to keep calm. If she went too crazy beforehand, she may not be able to state her case, and she had to. She looked over at the woman nestled into the bed that seemed to swallow her up in its massive size

"I'll, fix it Nana, I will." She whispered the words to herself. Her grandmother had been asleep for an hour now and a sounder sleeper you would never meet.

She caught a glimpse of herself in the mirror near the doorway. Her normally tamed head of hair was a jumbled mess. She was an average girl, at least she thought so. At 5'7 she was taller than many girls, she had dark green eyes and was in pretty good shape. She wasn't perfect by any means. She filled out her clothes nicely and was curvy. She was far from the model stick thin types most men preferred. Her hair was naturally curly and hung down past her shoulders.

There must have been 4 different shades of red mixed in there. Today what she needed most was some conditioner and a pony tail. She glanced over at the table where lunch had been placed and noticed a rubber band, it would have to do. With a shrug, she wrapped her hair in a severe bun and at least managed to contain the wild mess.

She took a seat by the large window in the room and opened a book. Reading calmed her and had always been a favorite pastime. There was something magical about being swept away into someone else's fantasy world. It made thing easier, especially when times got dark. She gave her Nana another look over. She had saved her life, literally. She owed her everything, and wouldn't stop short of giving her as much back. She would fix this mess, or die trying.

It had been twelve years since her life had changed for the better. At 26 there wasn't a day that went by that she didn't remember, and take time to appreciate the life she had now. Her mother had been an angry, bitter woman. That's pretty much all she could remember about her. She'd had Amelia young, they could have been sisters really. Her life had been hard and full of everything negative. Amelia could remember being hungry, and cold more often than not.

Her mother was always entertaining one man or another. Whatever money she made prostituting she would spend on drugs, throwing her son and daughter a crumb or two from time to time. When Amelia turned 10, things got even worse.

She felt the sadness well up in her, even now. Her brother's name was Evan. He was always a sweet boy, and often sick. He was younger by five years and Amelia tried her best to protect him. He never hurt anyone in his whole life and he could have been something wonderful. The day he disappeared was the longest day of her life.

Her mother was running late as always, and they were starving. She was only 10 years old, and she knew they could go to the neighbor's house and Miss Sinclair would help them. She was always giving them bread and candies. She had specifically told Evan to stay at the house. She had tucked him into the cot in their corner of the room and told him to wait and she would get them some food.

He had smiled up at her and she hugged him before going. It was the last time she would ever see him. Miss Sinclair wasn't home, but on her way back to their house someone had seen her, had followed her. He was a big man, he smelled of whiskey and smoke.

He grabbed her by the arm and refused to let go despite her kicking and screaming. With a kick to the groin, she had finally broken free and she ran, probably faster than she ever would again in her life. She made it home, and Evan was gone. She frantically looked for him, but there was no sign of him.

When her mother made it home finally she told her, but was ignored. Her mother just told her he was probably off playing somewhere. She felt helpless and lost, and she never wanted to feel like that again. Her thoughts were always with Evan, even now. Not long after the county had come and taken her away. She couldn't save him, but she could do something about her Nana.

There was something special in the air the day Lenora Randolph came to Bakerstown Girls Home. It may have been because her birthday was the day before or it may have been the way it was supposed to snow that week, which rarely happened in South Carolina. Whatever it was, you could almost feel it. Amelia had lived there for 2 years, and in her mind it was wonderful.

She had her very own bed and clothes and they always had food. When the people had put her here she had been scared, but over time she realized that it was wonderful. She didn't sleep at night for a long time, but gradually she had stopped having nightmares and now she felt more like everyone else.

There were always people coming there, looking to adopt a girl to love as their very own, but she never thought much about it. Babies and young girls were always the ones chosen. That was something she has been just fine with. Out there you never know who will come around, who will hurt you. Here she was safe. She knew everyone who worked there and she also knew they locked the doors every night. Inside the girls home, she didn't have to worry. It was a shock to her when a nice lady had come around to greet all of the older girls in her wing.

It was a rare occurrence and while everyone was putting on their best clothes she just went about her normal routine. Eventually the lady had asked her what her name was and the conversation they had that day changed her life forever.

"What is your name young lady?" The lady smiled at her as she sat down on the bed beside her.

"Me? My name is Amelia. How do you do?" she had thrust her hand out like she saw them do on television and the lady shook it in return.

"How are you doing today? I hear there is snow in the forecast." The lady had leaned over and smiled at her as they talked. Amelia smiled back, she was nice and she smelled like cookies.

"I'm okay. I guess. Sure is getting colder that's for sure, but I like it. I used to hate it when I lived out there and I didn't have heat, boy it was no fun at all. Now I hope to get to see some snow real soon." She went back to making her bed.

"It sounds like you have done a lot of stuff in your life, Amelia."

"I guess so, you see how everyone is running around and trying so hard to be their best? I just don't understand that at all. I just want to be me all the time, so I don't make anyone sad when they find out who I really am. That's why I ain't dressed up in the Sunday clothes. I hate to be a pest Ma'am, but could you stand up? I just have to get this bed made so I can get to breakfast. I am always hungry and I sure like to eat."

Amelia had given her a grin as the lady had jumped up quickly. She made her bed and gave the lady a hug before she headed down to the lunch hall.

"You sure smell nice, lady." Amelia skipped her way out of the room and thought nothing more of the situation, and the lady she had left upstairs.

Later that day the nice lady had asked her if she wanted to come live with her and at first she had said no. The lady had sat back on the chair in the library and watched Amelia for a moment before asking her why.

"It's not you lady, you seem real nice, honest. The thing is, there are a lot of bad people out there. Here they lock up the doors real tight and it's safe that's all. I guess, I just don't know how you do things. I don't want to get hurt like I did before. I don't want them to take me like they did Evan."

"Who is Evan, dear?"

She had leaned over and whispered. "I'm not supposed to talk about Evan. No one believes me about him. He was my brother and one day someone took him."

The lady had frowned for a second and told her. "Amelia, I can assure you one thing. I lock my house up every night, just like they do here. I am all alone in there and sometimes I want someone to talk to. I had a nice man who I was married to his name was Harold but he died and he is in Heaven now. I can't promise you won't ever get hurt again, the world is full of hurt, but I can promise I'll be there with you to help you through it."

She had frowned as she thought over what the cookie lady had said. She had locks, and she was sad too. Plus, she would have someone to help her and it was nice to hear someone say that. She would miss her friends here, but maybe she should go, the lady seemed real sad and maybe she could help her.

She smiled her best smile and agreed to go. She gathered up her small bag of things and with a deep breath she had walked out of the children's home and into the arms of her loving Nana. Her life had changed for the better, and Nana was the reason. She owed her so much and it was killing her to see her sick like this. Everything that she had gone through Nana had made it better, even if it was just a hug when the boy at school was mean to her or helping her by sitting with her through a panic attack.

Even now she still had those, when she couldn't be in control. Either way, her Nana fixed everything for her, she would do the same for her now. She glanced up at the clock in the room and sighed. She needed to work, that always helped keep her mind occupied. After another glance at her Nana she left to get some work done.

Jacob Montgomery worked hard and he deserved the nicer things in life. He wasn't cocky or overly confident. He didn't think he was some gorgeous Brad Pitt all women wanted. He did, however, think he was a good man, and he tried hard to do the right thing. It was the reason the mess he was in was so difficult.

He looked down at the picture in his hand and sighed. Amelia Randolph was becoming a problem he didn't want or need. He put the picture of the plant back down and raked his hand through his dark hair. Ever since the water had tested positive for some abnormal chemical content she had been blowing up his office day and night.

It wasn't that he didn't care, in fact, he was just as concerned as she was. The problem was she was a screeching, loud, demanding woman and he wasn't relishing the idea of having a meeting with her at all. There were steps that had to take place and he was only part of the board.

For whatever reason, she felt like somehow, it was all his fault. He had tried to call her back, only to get her voicemail, which in turn, had led to the meeting they were having on Friday morning. He wanted to give her the good news, for her grandmother's well-being, and to get her to stop leaving long winded, potty mouthed voice mails on his phone at work. He glanced out the long window in his office. It had been a long and windy road to get to this place.

At age 31 he had achieved more success than any other Montgomery before him. His great-grandfather had started this business and since then it had grown leaps and bounds. It had passed down to each Montgomery until now it rested on him. He could remember as a child watching his father, work the phones, spend his evening planning and most importantly dress sharp.

There was something about a great suit that made a man. Having something tailored to you was one of the luxuries he enjoyed as the CEO. He didn't drink, or do drugs and he worked effortlessly putting in long hours to make the business a success, and well, he liked nice suits. It gave him that extra push to do well and added to the confidence of representing the company well. It had started with his grandfather and one day he would pass this entire empire down to his children. That is, If he ever got married.

Jessalyn crossed his mind and he smiled. She was a wildcat if there ever was one. The wealthy daughter of a fashion designer they crossed paths on occasion and he had been taken in right away. She was a leggy blonde, her features almost too perfect, most likely due to a random number of surgeries. Despite the insincerity of her looks he liked her inquisitive nature and they had enjoyed each other's company for the last two years.

More often than not he would call ahead when he would be in town and she would make time for him, and vice versa. She was often away for modeling shoots and he was away for some business deal or another. On the rare occasion that their calendars would sync up they would get together and try to be "normal." She knew his world, the demands of it and never complained.

They never took things any deeper than a mutual respect and a great sex life. The last time he had seen her had been three months ago, and everything had changed. Somewhere along the way she had fallen in love with a model named Brutus and she couldn't meet for a rendezvous anymore.

He tried to gauge his feelings on it. He was stuck somewhere between relieved and lonely. He didn't have time for anything serious, and yet he hated never having anyone to spend time with. One of the benefits of that was that he had more time to focus on the task at hand, the water treatment system his company had installed a few towns over that could be making people sick. That brought his thoughts back to Miss Randolph and he cringed. It was going to be a long week, and an even longer Friday.

The weather in South Carolina has been never predictable. The winters would range from snow and ice to a mild 50 degrees. There was no understanding it really. The winter would fade easily into spring without much distinction and until you looked at a calendar there was no telling what month you were in at any given moment. Today was one of those chilly days where you wanted to go outside and take the day off, all bundled up.

Sadly, it wasn't meant to be for Amelia. She loved her job that wasn't the issue. What she loved more was her Nana and truth be told she didn't feel like she was doing much good. She loved the freedom her job gave her. She was a guardian and legal consultant for D.S.S. She traveled all of the time. She would often spend her days in Charleston then to Myrtle Beach.

Sometimes she would have a chance to go north for a few days. Wherever her work needed her, she would go. She loved working on each case, and was always thrilled when she felt like she was really helping a family. So many children were always left scared and alone. She could never go back, but she could move forward with change.

Today she was in Myrtle Beach meeting with a family, two children and abusive parents. It never got any easier when she met them for the first time. It just certainly helped when they gave her a smile. She took a deep breath and went through the double doors to the lobby where she would meet the children and the attorneys. He felt like he was somehow responsible for the entire mess. Each board member was currently looking down their respective noses at him across the table.

"Look Jacob, we understand this is a ...um... situation, however we have to follow protocol. I've managed to get with the investigation team and they are looking into the mess. I've heard you have a meeting with the Randolph family and I think you need to reel that in for us."

The comment came from Brandon Workman. He had been there as long as his father had.

"Listen, Workman I get what you're saying, I'm just not sure why I am the only dealing with P.R. Do we not have a team for that? I have my own business issues to work out with the Landowe project." A few of the people at the table glanced at each other and then to the table.

"Well, I'll be honest with you Jake, you're the spokesperson for these types of situations. You're the charmer, the good-looking guy. A situation like this takes finesse and strategy." He had the decency to blush slightly.

"Let me get this straight, I am the CEO and I am also a part-time playboy schmoozes the ladies in my off time?" He sat back in a huff.

Workman looked around the table at the other members before settling on Jacob again. "Well, yes so to speak. Your father was the same way before you. You both have that ability to put people at ease." He smiled slightly, the noisy throat clearing around the room didn't go unnoticed either.

"You mean with the women." He gave Workman a half smile. He was the voice of reason around here after all. "Fine I'll go at it alone, but I need some real results from the testing site before I walk into whatever mess comes with the Randolph lady."

Amelia stared at herself in the mirror in her old room. Today was going to be a long day. She was certain of that, and not much else. She had taken great care to look nice. Her hair was twisted up on the back of her head, her make-up was subtle and effective and she wore a nice suit and skirt. It fit her just right. She wore pumps, something she rarely did and she had a firm set to her jaw. Today she would get some answers. She stood and squared her shoulders and took a few deep breaths.

It was just like going into a new home. She would listen, make her assessment and they would go from there. She made her way down to the car and drove into town. It was a 25 minute ride into Charleston, just long enough that she could take in some deep breaths along the way and try to stop her heart from beating out of her chest. It would serve no purpose if she lost her temper, no matter what she had to stay calm.

She climbed the front stairs of the building and looked up at the massive structure. She shook her head. Who needed that much space for anything? It was all too much really. She entered and gave her name to the guard who patted her down with a wink and she was finally in the elevator going up. She heard a shout and she noticed a man running towards her so she thrust her hand out to stop the elevator. He slid into the elevator and took a deep breath.

"Wow, I barely made it that time, thanks." He glanced over at her. She was beautiful, her hair was a jumble of colors wound up tightly with the appearance that it would break free at any moment.

"Sure, no problem." She tried not to stare at him. He was reeking of sexiness. He had dark hair slightly unruly and blue eyes that felt like they could look a hole right through you. He was tall, very tall and impeccably dressed. She self-consciously ran her hands down over her skirt. She could feel him watching her and she finally turned to look at him.

"Is there something on my face or something?" She noticed his surprise and then the grin that slid into its place. "No, not at all, you're just beautiful, that's all." It was his turn to get a rise out of her. He saw the blush creep up her neck and into her face. "Whatever." She rolled her eyes and stared back at the elevator, watching intently as it made its slow accent to the top floor. "You are, but I have to say it is refreshing."

He failed to elaborate as the doors opened and he stepped out. "I hope to see you again." He whistled as he strode away from the elevator, leaving her wondering what he was talking about.

Men were crazy, that much she was sure of. Finally the elevator climbed the last few floors and she exited it into a massive waiting area. There was a coffee bar on one end of the room which looked like a small café. She couldn't believe the excess that people used. She made her way to the receptionist desk and gave her name.

"Randolph, you said Miss?"

"Yes, that's right." She noticed the receptionist glance around a bit before buzzing back to Mr. Montgomery's office.

"Yes, ok, yes that's fine, I'll let her know." She had glanced up at Amelia a few times before hanging up.

"Mr. Montgomery is on his way here now and as soon as he arrives I'll send you back."

With a huff, Amelia made her way over to an overstuffed chair in the lobby. He wasn't even there yet. The whole thing was ridiculous. He was probably on some yacht somewhere while her grandmother was lying in a hospital sick. She felt the tension rising and she hoped he would get there soon before anything else happened.

Jacob made his way up the stairs to his office. She had been a real beauty that one. She was gorgeous, but in an unrefined way and she was direct, something many people never were in his life, it made him like her even more. He was kicking himself for not getting her name at the very least. For now he would just have to hope he would run into her again soon. She was in his building how hard could it be to find one woman?

He gathered up some paperwork from his desk and made his way over to the conference room. The receptionist had already called him ten minutes ago and told him, Amelia Randolph was there. He knew what kind of morning as ahead of him, but he had exited the elevator a couple of floors down so that he could sneak up the back way.

He didn't need to be attacked in his own lobby. He quickly scanned the paperwork in his hands regarding the water testing site and frowned. This was not going to be a good meeting. At least he had chosen a conference room in the corner of the floor where they wouldn't be bothered, or heard. Reluctantly, he buzzed up front and told the girl to bring her in.

It was ridiculous how long someone had to wait for a meeting. The lack of attendance only solidified her opinion of Jacob Montgomery. If he had been a real gentleman, if he cared, he would have at least been on time. Finally the blonde called her name and escorted her to a room at the far side of the building. When she entered, she simply stared at the blonde shut the door.

"You! Really? Did you know it was me or do you always say things like that to people in an elevator?" She crossed her arms and stared at him as he stood.Equally stunned, and a little disappointed he thrust his hand out to her. "No, I didn't know it was you Miss Randolph." He gestured for her to take a seat.

She was upset, she'd be lying is she said that the mystery guy from the elevator had made her feel that warm fuzzy feeling you get deep down. To find out he was that ass, Montgomery she had been dreading squashed any thoughts she'd had while waiting in the lobby. To think, she actually hoped to run into him again, so she could apologize for being so gruff and to figure out what he meant by those last words. Now she was sitting face to face with him.

It was difficult to think straight with her sitting there staring at him. She was all fire and ice at the same time and he was intrigued. There was simply no way the squawking shrill voice on the voicemails could belong to this woman. He shook his head and decided to get down to business.

"Miss Randolph I am glad we were able to get together finally. I understand you have concerns over the new water treatment plant we have put in and I assure you I am working hard to figure out where the problem is." He sat forward looking at her intently.

"Listen, I know you think your gonna just give me some BS about the plant and how great it is. I don't want to hear any of that. The fact of the matter is people are getting sick, or in the hospital. Something is wrong and I am just here to find out what you are going to do about it before I start asking people myself." She leaned up in her chair meeting him eye to eye.

He almost couldn't stand it. She was on fire, and beautiful. He would be amused watching her come to life if it were in any other situation. He was not used to women like this, so full of fire. Typically a woman would be a hellcat from time to time, but that was in the bedroom. If they started out like this he could only imagine... Damn, he was getting sidetracked.

"I don't think you need to start asking anyone else, Miss Randolph. The fact of the matter is we have men down there working on it now. The most recent tests I have right here." He pushed the papers over to her. "As you can see there is nothing showing that the mineral content is above average. Although the levels are normal at the plant I am still concerned about why this happened to you. I have no intention of letting it go until I am sure we have fixed the problem, if there is one."

"All I know is that my Nana was fine and then the day after the water was running through your plant she started getting sick. She had been in the hospital three times and each time it's after she goes home and starts using your water." She pointed her finger at him for emphasis.

"I understand, Miss Randolph and I assure you there is nothing I won't do to make this right, for you." His eyes glittered at her dangerously as he emphasized the "for you." She felt the heat rush through her as he watched her. She cleared her throat and glanced back down at the paperwork on the able.

"This paperwork can say whatever it wants, the truth of the matter is something is wrong and I intend to find out what it is." She stood now and he rose with her.

"Fine, meet me at the plant tomorrow morning." He wasn't even sure what possessed him to say it. He knew very little about the mechanics of the plant itself, but he did have a full knowledge of the filtration system.

"What." She crossed her arms over her chest as she looked up at him.

"Tomorrow, meet me at the plant. I'll go take a look around myself and if you're there you can see things as they develop." He crossed his arms and the two of them stood facing each other for a long moment.

The whole thing was dangerous. She knew before she agreed that this was going to go badly. Despite the anger she held at the company, she was attracted to him. She hated herself for it. He stood casually waiting for her to give him an answer. He was probably used to women throwing themselves at him all the time and she would be damned if she was one of them. He was off limits and she needed to turn off whatever attraction she had. He was just a stuffy suit running a business that hurt her Nana. With renewed spirit, she looked up at him.

"Fine, I'll meet you there, what time." She said it with a deadly calm. Almost as if she was someone else. He didn't like this side of her, it made him take a step back.

"9 sharp. Does that work for you?" He took a small step towards her and watched the blush start to creep back up again. She felt it too, he was sure of it. "Sure, that's fine." She turned to leave and opened the door to the room and stopped as he called her name. "Yes?"

"Don't be late." He grinned as she shut the door with a bang and made her way out of the office.

Jacob Montgomery was a jerk, a total and unmistakable jerk. Not only that, he was arrogant and self-serving, just thinking about the way he stood there arms crossed without a care in the world made her want to scream. She rammed the car into gear and pulled out and headed to the hospital. She was still angry when she arrived.

Who did he think he was giving her orders anyway? She was a grown woman, almost as tall as he was and he thought he could just tell her what to do. Her family was the victim here. He was a bully, yes, that was it. He was just like those kids at the children's home who would give her grief the first year especially. They threw their weight around, uncaring about anyone else. Yep! Jacob Montgomery was a no good bully! She walked into her Nana's room to find her sitting up and chatting happily with the nurse.

"Nana you look great!" Her anger was gone in an instant. The turnaround was almost unbelievable. Yesterday she had looked so sick still and in the two nights she had been here she had done a complete turnaround.

"Amelia sweetheart, come give me a hug." She raised her arms up and Amelia hugged her tightly. She was so scared, every time she got better and went home the next time it would be worse.

"You must feel better Nana, I'm so glad. Every time you go home it makes you sick. It's that damn water system and I am working on getting it taken care of."

"Now, now Amelia we don't know that for sure yet. " She patted Amelia's hand lovingly and leaned back into her pillows. "I may look better, but I am terribly weak still. What have you been up to today, dear you are all dressed up?" She snuggled back into her pillow and shut her eyes momentarily.

"I had a meeting that's all. I met with Montgomery, to hash out things about the plant." She whispered it, in hopes Nana wouldn't really hear everything she said.

Her Nana's eye fluttered open. "You what! Oh Amelia it won't do it you get yourself all worked up. You know as well as I do that if you push too far you're going to get into trouble. Plus, we all know what happens with that temper of yours." She closed her eyes again, but not before giving Amelia a "You know what I mean" look.

"Yes, Nana I know all about my temper. In my defense, though I don't really get too upset unless I have a real reason to." She humbly looked down and started fighting with a string on the comforter covering the bed.

"Amelia, sweetheart, don't misunderstand I love all your fire, but just last week you made the poor paperboy cry." She gave a slight giggle before folding her hands over her lap.

"He was throwing the paper in the rose bushes Nana, how on earth can you climb in there and get it!"

Nana simply opened her eyes and gave Amelia a knowing glance. "I know, dear." She patted her hand one last time and Amelia watched as she was soon fast asleep.

Amelia sighed, it wasn't a lie. Her temper often got in her way. She liked to think that she was just passionate about certain things. Her work, her Nana and what was right. Besides, most of the time she was loud, but not angry. There was such a lack of common sense in some people she simply couldn't help herself. She made her way across the room and opened her tablet to look at her schedule.

She had a new family to work with next week, but the rest of this week she was free. She hadn't broached the subject of Nana coming to stay with her in her apartment yet. She knew it would be a fight.

Nana loved her house. It was where she and Harold had lived right after they got married and she had never stayed away from there unless she was in the hospital or when she had come to see Amelia graduate college in Maryland. It wasn't that she didn't understand.

The house had been here over half of her life. It was where she had learned to love, learned to trust again. It would always be a part of her life. She had to have Nana closer so that she could watch her more, be there if she needed anything.

Besides, her apartment was on the city water system in Ridgeville, not on the new "system" purchased from Montgomery Enterprises in Daniel Island. She could keep her safe if she would move in. She folded up her table and rested her head against the chair. She let her mind unravel the day's events and found herself fuming once more over the words of Jacob Montgomery.

She decided to get a room in town for the next few nights. It might be a huge expense, but she needed to be there early tomorrow, and the water was still in question at her Nana's, where she had been staying. She said her goodnights to Nana and made her way to a small and efficient hotel along the water. She had always enjoyed Charleston.

Even as a child she had loved the water, even when there was such a chill in the air like tonight. It was only mid-November and yet with temperatures like this maybe they would get some snow this year. The thought made her smile and think back about the snow when she had moved into Nana's house so long ago.

It was a long ride. It must have taken hours to get to the little white house, she was standing in front of. She looked up at the nice lady beside her who had decided to take her home. She took her hand. She was scared, but she didn't want her to know. She had left the girls home and she hoped this was going to be ok.

The nice lady patted the hand in hers and they made their way up the steps. When the door opened, she took a deep breath in of cookies and warm air. She loved being warm and full, both things she knew the nice lady said she never had to worry about again. She watched and waited as the lady locked the door behind her. It was only then that she relaxed.

"I've decided that maybe you should call me Nana. I'm not your mother, but I hope to be there to help you grow up. How does that sound?"

"Nana... I like it." She gave her a toothy smile and walked over towards a big picture on the wall of a man. "Who is he?" She hooked a thumb in the direction of the picture. Nana made her way over to her.

"That was my dear Harold. He went to Heaven a few months ago." She gently touched the picture and then turned to Amelia. "Well, dear are you ready to see your room?"

"I get my own room?" Amelia had gaped at her and followed along behind Nana. When she opened the door, she could just stand there.

The entire room was draped in pink and green. There were flowers on the large seat window and she had the softest pink blanket on her bed. There were pillows everywhere and Amelia rushed forward and immediately began to roll around the bed with them, giggling as she did. Nana laughed, pink may have been a bad choice this girl was not about to paint her nails all day she wanted to make a mess.

"The only thing left is to go buy you some clothes, we can do that tomorrow." Amelia ran to hug her close, happy for the first real time in her life. At some point that first night she had been overwhelmed by it all and snuck into Nana's room. She waited but a second before Nana pulled the blankets back. Without a word she had climbed in and snuggled down in the warmth of the blankets.

The snow came that weekend and the two of them played in the yard and built half of a snowman. She had laughed more in those two days than I her entire life combined. It's how her new life started and now that same chill was in the air tonight. She was still smiling when she put her bags on the floor of her room. She had a nice view and this would be a good way to make efficient use of the time she had. She locked and relocked the door.

A habit of sorts since she was a child. She let her thoughts stray to Evan. She had spent the better part of her career looking for him, some sign of him. She always came up empty. Every lead would bring some closure to another family, but never hers. She decided to take a shower and start prepping for her day tomorrow. There was no telling what Montgomery had up his sleeve.

So far all Jacob knew was that she wasn't married, and was adopted. He was scanning every piece of information about Amelia Randolph that he could. He needed to find something to connect them. To get her to relax some when he was around. She was 26, graduated from Maryland University. Worked at DSS on a flexible schedule.

She was practically broke, and had fairly good credit. He scanned her finances and noticed she spent a great deal of money looking for someone named Evan Hollinger. Whoever he was, she really wanted him found. Prior to age 12 there were no records for her. He sat back in his chair and spun to look out the window. Something about her fascinated him. Sure, she was beautiful, but that wasn't it.

He had been around beautiful women most of his life. Something wholesome about her made him want to know more. Whatever it was he was not giving up. He was used to getting and doing what he wanted and he wasn't going to start losing at the game now. She was all fire, and all talk. He would find a way to reach her and when he did, he would enjoy their time together. He smiled to himself before heading to take a shower.

The next morning was cold and gray. There was a bitter chill in the air that was hard to shake off. Amelia knew she needed to bundle up and she chose some casual clothes for the day. Denim and an oversized white sweater as well as her knee high leather boots. She put on her coat and hat, leaving her hair down for the extra layer of warmth. She glanced at the clock and swore. She was never late, ever. Why today of all days did she have to rush? She hastily grabbed her purse and made her way to her car. She didn't even have time for coffee that certainly added to her mood. She climbed in and turned the car over and nothing happened. She tried again.

"Really?" She said it out loud. The car had been giving her issues for a while now, but it was not the day. Of all days, not the day.

She jumped out of the car and shut her door with a bang. Now she would have to call someone and try and get the thing towed over to a garage. She hastily called Montgomery Enterprises.

After ten minutes of dealing with some snotty girl she passed on her message. He was probably laughing at her misfortune and happy she wouldn't be there to get in the way. She kicked the curb on her way back into her room and waited to hear from him.

Oh man, she was going to be angry, he smiled slightly thinking about her reaction. He wouldn't doubt it if she was kicking in the side of her car right now. He hung up his phone and looked around the penthouse for his coat. He decided to try and get on her good side and so he sent her a text asking where she was staying.

Perhaps there was some way he could put her back in a good mood before he arrived. He made his way downstairs and to his personal car. He liked to venture out on his own sometimes and today was the perfect day for it. He glanced up at the sky and frowned. It was probably going to snow later today. They weren't going to have much time if he didn't hurry. He pulled out onto the highway and made his way into town.

She was puzzled by his message, at least she assumed it was him. It wasn't like he had said "hey, it's Montgomery." She was frustrated by the whole situation and her lack of expertise when it came to cars. She needed to take a class or something. This was an awful situation to be in.

She saw him pull up before she even looked at who was driving. The red sports car was sleek and shiny and she knew it could only belong to Montgomery. She walked towards him from the lobby as he got out. He was handsome in black denim and a polo shirt. He had on a black coat and gloves, which he took off as he made his way over to her. He even had a sexy sway to his walk. She rolled her eyes, disgusted with herself.

He tried to gauge her mood as he made his way over to her. She had her arms crossed again, a sure sign she wasn't happy. Her jeans were tight, perfectly tight. She had rounded hips, he wanted to touch and her mane of hair flowed down past her shoulders. He wondered what it would feel like if he put his hands in it. Instead, he gave her a smile.

"I figured I could just pick you up and we go together. Saves time and gas."

"You could have told me you were coming. Or said who you were when you text me, you know?"

"Sorry, I was in a hurry." He frowned at her slightly. She really was always in a foul mood. "If you're coming I suggest we get going." He turned and headed towards his car.

She felt bad immediately. What was wrong with her, she was never this short tempered. She followed him to the car and slid into the seat, buckling up as he shut her door for her. She waited until she was inside before addressing the topic at hand.

"Listen Montgomery, I'm sorry. I don't know what's wrong with me. I'm just so concerned about Nana. This car situation just pushed me over. I appreciate the ride, really." She gave him a quick glance as he buckled up.

"My pleasure, and please call me Jacob. Using my last name reminds me of high school football. I don't want to revisit that." He grimaced slightly and she smiled.

They made their way to the water treatment plant near Daniel Island. It had been a huge undertaking for the company and he had overseen every aspect of the project. He had educated himself about the filtration process, but he wished now that he had learned more about the engineering of it. It was a gleaming metal unit attached on one side to the building that held the support offices and the staff who maintained it.

They made their way down and into the building. She had never been this close to it before and was in awe at the mechanics that went into running something of this magnitude. He asked for Benjamin Astren the manager of the plant and they were quickly greeted by a round man with a face as red as an apple. His happiness was almost infectious as he pumped both of their hands and led them into a control room. Most of what he said made no sense to her, but she took in every aspect of the system and how it worked.

"This channel here, do they lead strictly to Daniels Island or does it cover something else as well?" Both men turned her way and Benjamin answered.

"This filtration channel strictly runs to Daniels, more specifically the smaller end of Beresfor Creek. You can see the larger system pumps into the larger area of Beresford and then branches to Nowell Creek."

She looked over the system more before following them down towards the actual filtering controls. If the filtering channel ran strictly to Daniels Island than the issue would have to be central to that one run. She moved towards the huge pumping filters. They were massive and connected the water in the creeks into the system and then back into the holding tanks that would then pump water to the homes where they were directed. The whole set up was beautiful, even if it was making people sick.

"I have set up something for you both. I understand that there has been some concern on your part Miss Randolph about the water content. I have some instruments here, and if you would like to I'd be happy to allow you both to take your own samples and run them through the testing equipment. I think this could help with what you're looking for."

She smiled at him and readily agreed. They spent the next two hours moving and testing water both filtered and unfiltered. They talked about life in general, her work and his and she found that he really wasn't too bad to spend time around after all. He was still a rich snob, and a bully, but he wasn't as bad as she originally thought.

He was feeling the same way. She was a strong and smart woman and, unlike most women he knew, she didn't care that her clothes were wet and messy. She was on a mission and was all businesslike about it. She needed to know the truth. He loved the tinkling sound her laugh made when she wasn't trying so hard to be stern. He wanted to kiss her, right there with water spraying on them in the frigid air.

Even in these temperatures he was on fire thinking about it, about her. Eventually they were done and what they found left them both puzzled. There was no indication of any levels of negative or harmful properties in the water. What was being sent into Daniels Island was as pure as it could come.

What bothered him was the lack of an Hd5 filter he had specifically asked for on the system. It hadn't been put on the system and he had a pretty good idea why. The bored had fought him on the cost. They both left the plant lost in thought. After an audible sigh coming from her he glanced her way. She was upset and visibly so.

"I know you wanted, needed even, something to be there in that water. I had it tested over and over again. I also know, given your personality you wouldn't believe me unless you did the testing yourself."

"What do you mean my personality? Contrary to what you may think I am a very pleasant person to be around." He gave her a look with a half grin and she knew she was delivering him exactly what he had been referring to.

"Yeah, okay, I get it, I can be... difficult. It's just Nana, it doesn't make any sense at all Jacob. She is fine then goes home and then is sick again and everything they test at the hospital says it's in something she drinks. She only drinks water, I know that for a fact. That's all she has ever drank." She tapped her fingers on her lips in thought.

"I'm not sure what it is, but I'll continue to keep digging. I like it when you're not angry at me." He smiled at her again.

She felt the heat rising in her face. He had the most unusual ability to make her blush. She usually had a firm control on it. He turned left as they entered town and she frowned. This was not the way to the hotel. She felt the panic start building and she gripped the handle of the car door.

"Where are we going?" She gritted out the words. He turned to see her white faced and gripping the door. What was wrong?

"Hey, you ok? I was going to stop off for lunch, that's all. There is a diner right there see?" He pointed ahead and she could see the building. She relaxed and pulled her hand off the door handle.

"That's great, I'm starving." She gave him a weak smile and he frowned. Something was not right and he intended to find out what it was.

She excused herself to go to the bathroom once they were inside. She splashed some water on her face fighting the tears she didn't want to come. When would she ever stop being afraid? It wasn't often, but when the panic would set in, it was hard to shake off. Jacob wasn't going to hurt her, she knew that.

There was something about the day Evan had disappeared and the way the man had grabbed her. If he hadn't come along she might have made it home. She stood and used a paper towel to blot dry her face. She pushed her mass of hair back and pinched her cheeks for color. She frowned slightly. Was she really in here primping for Jacob Montgomery? She turned and made her way into the restaurant.

He noticed the color had returned to her face as she sat down. He continued to watch her as she ordered food and he gave her a smile once he had done the same. They made random small talk and he smiled again.

"What are you smiling at Jacob?" she leaned forward in the booth slightly.

"Nothing at all Amelia, I am appreciative of how you do things that's all."

She frowned again, that didn't sound very promising. "What do you mean how I do things?"

"I'm just used to women being a certain way that's all. I like you better." He flashed a smile at her again and she blushed.

"What's wrong with me that I'm not like other women?" The words were no sooner out of her mouth and the waitress delivered the food. She looked down at the massive meal before her. Chiliburger, fries, milkshake and cherry pie. She took a gulp and blushed as she looked up at him, "Point taken." His laughter was loud and she joined in with him.

"You are too much Amelia." He wiped at his eyes and started to attack the food on his side.

They hadn't been eating long when a leggy blond came into the diner. She gave a once over around the room until she found who she was looking for. Amelia knew trouble when she spotted it and this was definitely going to go badly.

The blond stopped at the table and made eye contact with Amelia. The two instantly disliked each other. The air surrounding the blond was enough to make you choke. She held her head up high and had a disgusted look on her face as she glanced around at the other patrons in the room.

"Jacob, darling." She said it sweetly and he gave a start as he glanced up at her.

"Jessalyn, wow, what are you doing here?" He stood up quickly and glanced over at Amelia.

"I called the office and they said you were stopping here on your way back, I had to see you darling, and something important has come up." She looked down her nose at Amelia before adding. "Darling, what are you doing in a place like this?"

He gritted his teeth and introduced the two. "Jessalyn this is Amelia, Amelia, Jessalyn."

"Nice to meet you." Amelia managed to get out. She received a half smile from her counterpart.

"Jessalyn, now is not a good time we are working on some business together and I'm driving."

"Really Jacob we need to talk, it looks like there is another person here with you, " she gestured at all the food on the table, "Can they not take her home, I really need to chat with you." She felt the sting of the words and noticed he had the decency to look angry.

Before he had a chance to make it worse, she decided to chime in. "Jacob its fine, I can find my way to the hotel, it's just around the corner.

Go its fine." She leaned back in the chair, noticing the pained look on his face.

"No, it's not right here." He threw her his keys. "Drive it to your hotel and I'll come get it later. I'll just ride with her." Before she could turn him down he left and escorted blondie with him.

It wasn't really about what she said. It was really about how this woman was the type Jacob was obviously interested in. She never wanted to be like that. She would take her jeans and a chili burger every day of the week before she would show up and look down her nose at the world. She finished her lunch and decided to take the sports car for a ride to the hospital. The rest of the evening flew by for them both.

Jacob's head was reeling and he wasn't sure what he was going to do. Jessalyn had come back here just to tell him she may be pregnant. The last thing he needed was a baby with a woman he didn't love. It changed his entire thought process. If it was his of course he would be a good father. There was nothing more important than that. She was going to the doctor tomorrow and then he would know what was going on.

He looked over at his clock. 8 pm. Amelia was probably wondering when he was coming to get his car. He loved that car, he was still surprised he had given her the keys. He tried to call her but no answer. He smiled. She had been carefree and relaxed. He liked her that way. Whatever had caused her to panic in the car is what concerned him. Something wasn't right there and he decided to look into it. He sat forward and opened his computer.

Her back was killing her. All she could think of was the pain she was feeling and her eyes flew open to investigate the culprit. She was draped across the chair in Nans room and the blanket someone had draped over her had twisted itself into the nuisance currently digging into her back. She glanced at the clock and yawned. It was 10 o'clock. She needed to get back to the hotel.

She felt around the table for her keys and frowned at the weight of them. Suddenly her eyes opened wide. She still had his car. Damn.

She jumped up carefully tiptoeing out of the room and rushed out to the car. She slipped into his cool leather seats. It was only then that she noticed the snow was falling. She grabbed around for her phone and noticed he had called. She decided to text him in case he was asleep.

"Fell asleep, sorry. Your car is at my hotel whenever you want it."

She carefully made her way through town with a smile on her face as the snow fell gently in waves. She had just pulled into a spot and jumped out when she heard something behind her. She stopped.

"Hey beautiful come hang out with me." He was drunk and walking towards her car. He was halfway between her and the hotel. She grabbed her purse and started to run past him. He reached out and grazed her arm and she went into a full panic. She sprinted past him and ran into something hard and warm. She looked up and Jacob was the last thing she saw before she fainted.

Warmth. She always loved it. She snuggled down into the blankets and sighed. She had been having the most wonderful dream about Jacob kissing her. Jacob! She sat up with a start. The last thing she remembered was looking up at him.

"Hey there sleepyhead." He was comfortably draped out in a chair beside her bed and reading through some paperwork. She looked over at the clock. It had only been an hour since she left the hospital.

"What happened? What happened to that man did he leave?" She was frantic now and shaking like a leaf. He walked towards her and wrapped her in a hug.

"He is gone, Amelia, I called the police and he is gone." He felt her relax in his arms. She smelled like lavender.

He wanted nothing more than to stay just like this. She raised her head to look at him and it was more than he could take. He crushed his mouth to hers. Tasting and exploring. He had wanted to kiss her since the elevator and it was better than he had expected. He felt her let go and he deepened the kiss. He slid both hands into her hair and pulled

"Yeah, because I'm so skinny I may just float away." She said it with sarcasm and a smile.

"I don't like skinny, I like curves." He glanced at her and crossed his arms, "You'll do." She threw a pillow at him as she wound her hair up in a ponytail and sat down to eat a quick breakfast.

"So you have an answer about what?" She sipped her coffee and ate her food.

"Oh no, it's a surprise, just eat and we will go." He gave her a huge smile as she licked her fingers clean. She was adorable.

"What?" She shrugged. He handed her a coat and they made their way to the car.

As they rode along she thought it was a good time to bring up last night."Jacob listen. Last night was great. I don't want you to worry I will be expecting anything. I hope we can be friends and everything." She watched the trees fly by as she said it.

"What are you talking about? Expect anything? This isn't high school, Amelia.

"I'm just saying..."

"I know exactly what you're saying." He cut her off and she frowned. She had given him an out, and he was pissed. She glanced back out the window and frowned, they were headed to her Nana's house, she was sure of it. He made the final turn and pulled into the driveway of her childhood home."Jacob what are we doing here?" She got out and waited as he pulled a large bag out of the trunk.

"I was thinking, your Nana was getting sick when she was at home drinking, but the water tested fine at the plant. The only solution is the pumping system here at the house."

They made their way around the house to the old water cover and pump. She knew factually it hadn't been changed or looked at in at least 12 years. He pulled the cover off the system and turned on the water directly coming out of the pipe. He put some in a vial and put two drops of something in it and shook. It took less than a minute before theater turned a dark blue color.

"I knew it, the lead levels are through the roof. The problem is the system outside the house Amelia."

She took the vial from him in awe. All this time she had been coming after him and the problem was, literally, in the backyard. She made her way inside and he followed. She sat at the kitchen table and rested her head in her hands. Now she would get it fixed, and everything would go back to normal.

"How much does one of those things cost?" She glanced over at him as he looked around her old room. "It varies really, not too much." He smiled at her.

"Listen, I don't know what I said earlier, but I was trying to make it easy for you to walk away, you get that right?" She crossed her arms over her chest. Something she had done many times before.

"Amelia, I don't want to be let off the hook, I want you, I want to be there for you when it gets hard, I want to eat chili burgers together and be close if you panic again, and you don't have to be scared of anything ever again." He took a step towards her and she frowned.

"What are you talking about? Panic again or scared anymore?" She looked up at him and her face fell. "Did you look up information about me, Jacob?"

He looked scared before he answered. "Yes, but I wanted to get to know you that's all I didn't know about, everything you had been through."

"So you found out all about me and then slept with me? What was the reason, pity?" She was loud now, angry and crying.

"Amelia, no, it's not like that. He took a step towards her."

She stopped him, "Go Jacob, just go. NOW!"

Nothing left to say he made his way outside and spun his tires as he headed back to Charleston.

She had been back to work two weeks now. She tried to take on every case she could, to help take her mind off of things. Two weeks since she had seen him. He was still texting and calling and she refused to acknowledge any of it. He had betrayed her. She looked up from her desk.

Tonight she would go see her Nana and check on the new system she had purchased with a new credit card. It would take at least a year to pay it off, but it was worth it. She made her way to her car and set off for Daniel Island.

This had to work, he had tried everything else and yes, it was sneaky getting Nana in on it but she wouldn't respond to him. He was in love with her and she loved him too, if she would stop being so stubborn. He had hurt her, he knew that now, but he couldn't make it right if she avoided him.

He glanced over at Nana who was rocking happily in her chair. They had talked for hours about Amelia and she knew he loved Amelia very much. She had shared so much about Amelia he loved her even more than he had before. He stood when he heard the car pull up. She was going to be furious, and he knew it.

"She will only be mad for a moment son, she is always more bark than bite." Nana chuckled to herself.

The door opened and she came in with an armful of bags. "Nana what in the hell is that monstrosity out back? I didn't pay for that and I hope they don't think I'm going to. That model was $5,000 more dollars than the one I got you. Not that I don't want you to have the best but ..." She trailed off as she turned and saw him there.

"Don't get mad, don't say anything until I'm done Amelia." He glanced at Nana who gave him an encouraging nod. Amelia stood frozen to the spot. "I am in love with you Amelia Randolph and I probably was from the first day we met. I know what I did was wrong, I'm sorry if I hurt you. The truth is we belong together.

You help me be a better man and I'll force you to go to society balls and spend a lot of money on charities and things you will hate doing, but you will do it because you love me. I want to spend my life with you Amelia, and I want to face challenges together. I want to help you find Evan."

He looked over at her and the tears streaming down her face. Good or bad he wasn't sure yet. Nana, who always loved a good love story sat up on the edge of her seat and waited. With a sob Amelia threw herself into his arms and relished in the feel of him holding her. This was where she belonged. She looked up at him.

"That monstrosity out there I bought for Nana. She deserved the best. She brought us together, it was the least I could do." He gave Nana a grin and she just shooed him away. He hugged her close.

"Do you remember in the elevator that day, I said it was refreshing?" He smiled.

"Yes, what did you mean exactly?" She pulled away slightly.

"I meant it was refreshing to meet a woman who was beautiful and didn't even know it." He leaned in for a kiss.

****

Don't miss out!

Visit the website below and you can sign up to receive emails whenever J.L. Ryan publishes a new book. There's no charge and no obligation.

https://books2read.com/r/B-A-FWWB-CPDT

BOOKS 2 READ

Connecting independent readers to independent writers.

Also by J.L. Ryan

Alpha Billionaire Club Boxed Set
Bad Boy Billionaire Boxed Set
Billionaire Obsession
Billionaire Protector
Billionaire Scandal
Irresistible: A 7-Book Billionaire Romance Boxed Set
Owned by the Billionaire: A 5-Book Billionaire Romance Boxed Set
Plus Size Romance: A 9-Book Billionaire Romance Boxed Set
The Billionaire's Offer
Billionaires and Bad Boys
Billionaire Unleashed Boxed Set Series
Billionaire Unloved
Seduced by the Billionaire: A 5-Book Boxed Set
The Billionaire CEO: 4-Book Boxed Set
Curvy Romance
The Billionaire's Gift
The Billionaire Boss
Heart Of The Billionaire
BBW Romance
Baby For The Billionaire
Alpha Male Romances: 4-Book Boxed Set
BBW Curvy Romance: A 16-Book Boxed Set
BBW Romance
BBW Romance With Billionaires Box Set
Alpha Billionaire Club Boxed Set: 11-Book Boxed Set

Bad Boy Billionaire: A Billionaire Steamy Romance
Billionaire: A Box Set Book Series
Billionaire BBW Romance
From Agony To Ecstasy: A Billionaire Romance Boxed Set
Bad Boy Alphas Boxed Set
Heart Of The Billionaire
BWWM Billionaire: A Billionaire Romance Series
The Billionaire's Surrogate
The Billionaire's Virgin Surrogate
BDSM: The Billionaire Dom's Submissive Surrogate
Anatomy Class
Billionaire Daddy
The Billionaire's Secret Baby
Saved By The CEO: A Steamy Billionaire Romance
Billionaire Love Story